THE CINDERELLA KILLER

A Charles Paris Novel

Simon Brett

CRÈME de la CRIME

This first world edition published 2014
in Great Britain and the USA by
Crème de la Crime, an imprint of
SEVERN HOUSE PUBLISHERS LTD of
19 Cedar Road, Sutton, Surrey, England, SM2 5DA.

Trade paperback edition first published
in Great Britain and the USA 2014 by
SEVERN HOUSE PUBLISHERS LTD.

British Library Cataloguing in Publication Data

Brett, Simon author.
  The Cinderella killer. – (A Charles Paris mystery)
  1. Paris, Charles (Fictitious character)–Fiction.
  2. Murder–Investigation–England–Eastbourne (East
  Sussex)–Fiction. 3. Actors–Fiction. 4. Pantomime
  (Christmas entertainment)–Fiction. 5. Detective and
  mystery stories.
  I. Title II. Series
  823.9'2-dc23

ISBN-13: 978-1-78029-064-5 (cased)
ISBN-13: 978-1-78029-546-6 (trade paper)

Typeset by Palimpsest Book Production Ltd.,
Falkirk, Stirlingshire, Scotland.

To
Caro,
with love and thanks for directing
my pantos so sympathetically

ONE

FAIRY GODMOTHER: So welcome! Everything is grand
In good Prince Charming's happy land!

'Sure, I know what pantomime means,' asserted Kenny Polizzi.

'Really?' said Charles Paris.

'Hell, yes. It's all that whiteface shtick, isn't it? Stuff that kids at theatre school do, before hopefully growing out of it. Pretending they're locked in boxes and feeling their way out, leaning against invisible bars, garbage like that. Who's that French guy who did it all the time? Marcel Somebody?'

'Marcel Marceau. But no, that's not pantomime. That's mime.'

'Pantomime – mime – what's the difference?' The large man shrugged. He seemed unaware that everyone in the Sea Dog pub in Eastbourne, while pretending not to, was looking at him. Maybe he genuinely hadn't noticed. More likely, it seemed to Charles, Kenny Polizzi was just used to being recognized everywhere he went.

He was the star of the American sitcom *The Dwight House*. Though the show had been discontinued some five years previously, so many episodes had been made during its glory years that there wasn't any time day or night when one wasn't being screened somewhere in the world. Dwight Bredon, as played by Kenny Polizzi, had the same kind of brand recognition as Ronald McDonald.

He was trimmer than he had been in *The Dwight House* years. His formerly ample figure had suited the slightly slobbish character of Dwight Bredon, whose house was home to his children from three marriages and, as the writers became increasingly desperate for storylines, any number of cousins, school friends, waifs, strays, dogs, cats, gerbils and even an alien.

Though Kenny Polizzi was probably about the same age as Charles Paris himself, in his late fifties, his body's contours suggested habitual attendance at a gym (not a venue ever frequented by Charles). The gingerish wig he wore exactly copied the style adopted by Dwight Bredon in all those many episodes. It was a very good wig, though not so good that Charles was left in any doubt it was one. Having been an actor for so long, his antennae for unnatural hair enhancement were particularly sensitive. He was fortunate still to have a good covering on top of his head, so Charles Paris only wore wigs when – as female actors say when justifying taking their clothes off – 'the script demanded it'.

His hair was getting increasingly grey at the temples – still hopefully just on the side of *distingué* rather than decrepit – and he hoped when the grey had colonized all of his head he'd resist the temptation to dye it. So far as Charles could see from the evidence of other actors, the only tint available for men was the colour of conkers. And he didn't fancy going around looking like that. He had his pride.

Charles was drinking a large Bell's with ice. Kenny had a sparkling mineral water, without even ice or lemon. Though he had been through the phases of hellraising, alcohol and other substance abuse required for the CV of a major star, all that was now apparently behind him. The body of the new squeaky clean Kenny Polizzi was a temple (whereas that of Charles Paris was more like a small deconsecrated chapel in need of restoration).

Kenny had just arrived in England. He had been due the previous day, Monday the twenty-sixth of November, for the first rehearsal for the Empire Theatre Eastbourne's Christmas production of *Cinderella*, but a terrorist alert had closed Heathrow. As a result he'd arrived in a limo at the end of the second day's rehearsal, by which time the producer, director and most of the cast had left. So the limo had drawn up at the rehearsal venue, St Asaph's Church Halls, virtually next door to the Empire Theatre, to find only one young harassed stage manager.

She knew it was a fairly safe bet that Charles Paris would be in the Sea Dog, so she had taken the American star to meet him there, while she tried to sort out what had happened to the PR company who were meant to be looking after him.

Given all these upheavals, Kenny was remarkably laid-back and gracious. Many considerably smaller stars might by this stage have been stamping their little feet and throwing their toys out of the pram, but Kenny seemed almost serene about the delays and disruptions.

When Charles mentioned this, he was rewarded by a Dwight Bredon smile and the words, 'Man, I just needed to get outta the States. Now I'm outta the States everything's cool.'

'And it was the prospect of acting in *Cinderella* that lured you away?'

'Charles, I didn't need no luring. I was gagging to get away. I told the agent, "Find me some work, as far away from Hollywood as you can get it." He came up with *Cinderella* in Westbourne – great.'

'Eastbourne.'

'Whatever. Just so long as I'm outta the States.'

'You make it sound like you're on the run from the Mafia,' said Charles with a chuckle.

Kenny's eyes narrowed. And with a new level of seriousness he said, 'You might not be a million miles from the truth there.'

Charles was a little shaken. Was Kenny joking? Or was he serious? Probably not the moment to dwell on Mafia connections, so Charles asked, 'So you really don't know what pantomime is?'

'I told you – it's black tights and white faces.'

'No, it isn't. Didn't you ask your agent what you were letting yourself in for?'

'I did not. I just checked with Lefty that the money was OK – which it is – and got on a plane. Or rather didn't get on a plane till twenty-four hours later because Heathrow was closed.'

Charles looked at his watch. 'Your car'll be here soon to take you to the Johnny Martin recording.'

'Is that a big show?'

'Probably our most popular late-night chat show. Used to just be on a Friday and pre-recorded as live. Now it's three nights a week, still pre-recorded, though, a few hours before it goes out.' Kenny nodded with satisfaction. 'And Bix thinks it's important you know a bit about pantomime before you talk to Johnny.' Charles referred to *Cinderella*'s director, the former choreographer Bix Rogers.

'Sounds reasonable. But it can't be that difficult. We're

talking *Cinderella* here, aren't we? I know *Cinderella*. Everyone knows *Cinderella*. If you're my age, there's no way you got through grade school without having seen *Cinderella*.'

'You're talking about the Walt Disney version?'

'Sure. Is there any other one?'

'In pantomime there are quite a lot of other ones.'

'OK, tell me about them.'

'Well, the basic story is much the same as the one you know. Cinderella is the downtrodden youngest daughter of three, and the older two are her Ugly Sisters – stepsisters, actually. She wants to go to Prince Charming's ball, but—'

'Charles, I know this stuff.'

'Yes, I'm sure you do. But what you don't know is that in pantomime Prince Charming is played by a girl.'

'A girl?'

'And the two Ugly Sisters are played by men.'

'Yeah?'

'And then Dandini, who's Prince Charming's friend, is usually played by a girl too.'

Kenny looked dubious. 'So pantomime's some kind of kinky transgender thing? It's not going to do my image much good to get involved in—'

'No, pantomime's the ultimate all-age entertainment. Part of the regular Christmas ritual for many British families.'

'Oh.' Kenny thought for a moment, then asked anxiously, 'Does this mean I'm going to have to drag up for the show?'

'No, no. The character of Baron Hardup is a man, and he's played by a man.'

'Thank the Lord for that. And where does he fit into the story?'

Charles was surprised by how little Kenny seemed to know about the job he'd agreed to take on. 'He's Cinderella's father. And of course stepfather to the Ugly Sisters too.'

'Is he one of the good guys?'

'Yes. I've played the part. It's quite fun.'

'When did you play it?'

'Oh, years ago.' Charles thought nostalgically of that production in Worthing. And of Jacqui, the dancer who was playing A Villager, White Mouse and Court Lady (for the Finale). He had fond memories of the time they'd spent together back then. No commitment on either side, just very nice sex for the duration of the run. He had less fond memories of the review his performance had received from the *Worthing Herald*. 'Charles Paris played Baron Hardup, and lost.'

'So what does the Baron do?' asked Kenny.

'He often gets involved in the slapstick routines with the Ugly Sisters.'

'Slapstick? Hell, I thought that went out with the Three Stooges.'

'It lives on in pantomime. It's one of the traditions.'

'Are there a lot of these traditions, Charles?'

'You bet. Built up over three centuries. Where shall I start? As I said, there's the slapstick scene. Then there's the transformation scene, and at the end you have special costumes for the Walkdown. And there's the audience-participation song, for which the song sheet is brought down from the flies. The Good Fairy always enters stage right, the Demon stage left. Then there'll be a "Behind you!" exchange with the audience, and at least one "Oh yes, it is!/Oh no, it isn't!" routine. And of course don't let's forget the pantomime horse, where one person's the front and one's the back.'

'You're kidding me,' said Kenny Polizzi.

Charles Paris didn't normally watch chat shows. He found that the guests rarely had anything interesting to say, and when they were actors it just rubbed in how much more successful than his their careers were.

But he did watch the *Johnny Martin Show* that evening. He wanted to see how much Kenny Polizzi had taken in from his crash course in the mysteries of pantomime.

In the event Johnny and his star guest said very little about the subject. There was a statutory plug in the intro, the news that Kenny Polizzi would be opening in *Cinderella* at the Empire Theatre, Eastbourne on Friday the seventh of December, running till the middle of January, but that was it. There was much more interest in the glory days of *The Dwight House*.

Johnny Martin was a very straight, almost old-fashioned, interviewer. The vogue for outlandish gay comedians fronting chat shows – and making the encounters more about them than about their guests – seemed to be on the wane. Which was very good news as far as Charles Paris was concerned. Johnny Martin's approach, by contrast, was in the traditional style pioneered by David Frost, Michael Parkinson and Terry Wogan. His research was impeccable, he cued his guests seamlessly to wheel out their well-oiled anecdotes and could almost be said to take a back seat during his interviews. It was a refreshing change after the rash of egotistical exhibitionists who seemed to Charles to have commandeered the air waves recently.

But Johnny Martin was not a complete pussy cat. He was very good at soft-soaping his guests, lulling them into a sense of serene bonhomie and then snapping a controversial question at them. Whatever agreements might have been made before about the subject-matter for interview, Johnny would disregard them. He was particularly adept at this method with politicians. He knew all MPs love appearing on television and love even more talking about things other than politics, their hobbies and little quirks that make them come across as regular, normal, even nice people.

Then, just when the discussion was at its cosiest, Johnny would throw in a barbed dart of a question which really got under his interviewee's skin. Some issue of an expenses irregularity, a well-paid consultancy with a company of dubious morality, an inappropriate closeness to a lobbyist, the hint of a sexual misdemeanour . . . these would suddenly be raised without any change in the mask of the interviewer's bland smile.

As a result, though politicians always preferred appearances on chat shows to programmes of serious debate like *Newsnight*, quite a few of them chose never to appear on *The Johnny Martin Show* for a second time.

The host's early questions about *The Dwight House* were predictably lightweight. Johnny catalogued the show's amazing statistics, the awards it had won, the stars whose careers had been quick-started by appearances as Dwight Bredon's children, the number of countries round the world it had been sold to.

Kenny Polizzi was used to this routine. He had a few finely honed humorous responses to these familiar facts. He said what a privilege it had been to work on the show, how no one knew at the start the huge showbiz phenomenon it would become, how the whole company had been like one happy family, and how *The Dwight House*'s success had had nothing to do with him. It had been a team effort and though he was the show's figurehead, he would never forget the important contribution made by every single individual connected with it.

This was all standard stuff, much of which Kenny had wheeled out in various award-collecting moments. It was bland and self-congratulatory, but he managed to inject a little of the bewilderment which had been so much part of his character in the show. Dwight Bredon was a lovable goofball, a man to whom things happened, who was in a state of constant surprise at events erupting around him. Cleverly, Kenny gave the impression that that was what had happened to him too. He's just been standing there, doing nothing in his usual way, and he'd been offered the part. And he was still a little in shock from all the wonderful things that had followed from that initial piece of good fortune.

What came across to the audience of *The Johnny Martin Show* was exactly what was intended to come across. Kenny Polizzi was a regular guy who you'd happily meet in a bar and have a beer with. There was no side to him. And given the scale of his international success, he remained a very modest man.

It was then, just when interviewer, interviewee and audience had achieved the cosy warmth of a friendly chat, that Johnny Martin threw in the first of his loaded questions.

'Kenny, I must say you're looking very fit.'

'Well, thank you for that, Johnny. I have been working out a bit. I have this very good personal trainer back in the States, and he's worked out a programme that I'll be following while I'm over here. Yes, I'm glad to say I am very fit.'

'And very clean?' asked Johnny slyly.

But Kenny wasn't going to be caught out that easily. 'Perfectly clean, thank you. I shower regularly – as I hope you do too.'

This got a friendly laugh from the audience, but it did not divert Johnny from his line of questioning. 'I was meaning "clean" in the sense of "clean from all substance abuse".'

'Well, I'm clean that way too.'

'Good news.' A little pause. 'Because that wasn't always the case, was it, Kenny?'

That he was annoyed by this was shown by the slightest change of expression, so minimal that only a behavioural psychologist – or a fellow actor – would have picked up.

'What're you saying here?' asked Kenny Polizzi.

'Just that you had a reputation in the past for being a bit of a hellraiser.'

'I don't know about a hellraiser. I did have a reputation in the past for being considerably younger than I am now. But I guess that goes for all of us, Johnny boy.'

'So how long have you been completely free of drugs?'

It was a question so leading that it would not have been allowed in any British court of law, but Kenny was wise to it. 'I've been free of any but prescription drugs since I emerged from my mother's womb.'

'What about alcohol?'

'I don't recall there being any around in the maternity suite.'

That got a big laugh. Unusually, Johnny Martin was being turned over in the contest. And he didn't like it. 'Kenny, there were lots of rumours in the gossip columns about you partying rather heavily and—'

'Sure, I liked to party. Name me an actor who doesn't. I dare say even you in your time have been something of a party animal, Johnny boy.' Having coined the diminishing nickname, Kenny was going to stick with it.

'Well, I, er . . .'

'Anyway, do you believe stuff you read in the gossip columns? If you believed everything that's been written about me, then you'd think I was a drug fiend and alcoholic who's been to bed with every woman in Hollywood.'

'Is that not true?'

'No, I couldn't manage *all* of them.'

It was a good riposte. Again it made Johnny look silly. And the implication was there that, although Kenny hadn't bedded *every* woman in Hollywood, he'd had his way with a good many of them.

'So your hellraising days are behind you, are they, Kenny?'

'You could say that . . .'

'I just did.'

'. . . but because there never were any hellraising days, it's kinda hard to put them behind me.' There was a twinkle in the actor's eye; he was actually teasing his inquisitor.

'So how long is it since you last had a drink, Kenny?'

'If you'd been looking, Johnny boy, you'd have noticed that I've just had a sip from your excellent water on the table right here.'

'I meant an alcoholic drink.'

'Well, you should have said that, shouldn't you, rather than confusing me?'

'How long is it, Kenny, since you had an alcoholic drink?'

'It'll be two years on Thursday.'

The directness and the seriousness with which this was said almost threw Johnny. The audience applauding the feat did little to settle him either. He stumbled a little over saying, 'Congratulations,' then moved on. 'And may I ask your current marital status, Kenny . . .?'

'I am currently unmarried.' He turned to face his public. 'Footloose and fancy-free. On the market once again. *Available.*' This was greeted by some raucous shouts and cheers from the female members of the audience.

'But you have been married?'

'Don't know why you bother asking me that question, Johnny boy. You know the answer. Or if you don't, it doesn't say much for your researchers.' Kenny was virtually taking over the interview now. 'Yep, I've had four marriages. I should be getting good at it by now.'

'And have you got a fifth Mrs Polizzi lined up?'

'Still sorting out the final paperwork on the divorce from the fourth.'

'That being Lilith Greenstone?'

'Yes, your researchers have been doing their stuff.'

'She's almost as big a star as you are.' Polizzi shrugged. 'And seems to be rather busier than you are at the moment. Was that one of the problems with the marriage – that her career was doing rather better than—?'

'I'm not going to say anything about Lilith in public. If I do one of her lawyers might hear it and screw another coupla million dollars out of me.'

'You say you're currently fancy-free, but you have been seen at some Hollywood events recently escorting the lovely British actress Ann Jordan. Is there anything there?'

'There's a very pretty girl there. Who I happen to know. But if I married every pretty girl I happen to know . . . hell, I'd have to have a camp bed at the wedding chapel.'

'So you're not going to tell us any more about you and Ann Jordan?'

'Dead right I'm not, Johnny boy.'

'Hmm.' The host recognized he wasn't going to get any further there, and did something almost unprecedented. He looked at his notes before starting on a new tack. 'Kenny, there's been a lot of controversy recently over American gun laws.'

'Sure.' His expression showed he was ready for this one too.

'And you know that over here we have rather different views on the right of citizens to bear arms.'

'Uh-huh.'

'You have your Constitution . . .'

'And the Second Amendment, yeah.'

'And you have spoken out in public in support of your current gun laws . . .'

'I have.'

'And I believe you have quite an extensive collection of guns . . .'

'Yup. With some folks it's stamps or butterflies. With me it's guns.'

'Well, Kenny, now you're in England, do you wish you had the right to carry a gun here?'

It was a good question, just controversial enough to allow Kenny Polizzi to show himself up. His reply could have quite an effect on his image this side of the pond.

'Well, there's a bit of me – a bit of most Americans, Johnny boy,' he said, 'that always feels kinda naked without a gun. But the United States, I'm sorry to say, is still quite a violent place. The only reason I need a gun over there is because everyone else I meet will also have a gun.' Ingenuously, he spread his hands wide. 'Self-protection. Whereas here in this cute little island of yours it's only the bad guys who got guns. What use would I have with a gun over here? What could I use it for? To stir my afternoon tea with before I make a start on the cucumber sand-wiches – what-ho?'

He said this last sentence in the English accent of a Wodehousian silly ass. The *Johnny Martin Show* audience loved it.

And back in his digs in Eastbourne, Charles was also impressed by Kenny Polizzi's media savvy.

TWO

FAIRY GODMOTHER: Now I will use my magic arts
To summon help from foreign parts.

As he was about to enter the rehearsal room, Charles Paris looked at the new *Cinderella* poster with practised cynicism. Since time immemorial 'billing' – literally where your name appears on the playbill and in what size lettering – has been very important to actors. It's the kind of detail their agents wrangle about endlessly with managements (or they do if their agent is someone other than Charles's – Maurice Skellern).

And the rule of thumb is that the more the performer is being paid, the more prominent he or she will be on the poster. In the theatre, billing is an unarguable reflection of success or failure. The highest peak attainable is a position 'above the title'. The artiste who reaches that level is an undoubted star, more important than anyone else in the show, more important than the show itself (and certainly more important than the show's writer).

But then sometimes a show has two stars, each of whom has the right to appear in that coveted position. In that situation the wrangling between agent and management becomes even more heated.

The *Cinderella* poster left no doubt as to who was the star. The size of Kenny Polizzi's name suggested that he must be being paid about fifty per cent of the production's budget. This implication was endorsed by the way his photograph dominated the space. The internationally recognized face of Dwight Bredon beamed out, a tribute to expensive dental work, five times the size of any of the other cast pictures. He was dressed in a shabby eighteenth-century frock coat, whose slight misalignment suggested that his head might have been superimposed on the costume by some photographic wizardry. And below his name was the legend: 'As Baron Hardup'.

The poster was new because of his relatively late booking.

Earlier versions had been dominated by the names and photo-graphs of two British soap stars. Cinderella was being played by Tilly Marcus 'from TV's *Gatley Road*' while one of the Ugly Sisters, Nausea, was to be Tad Gentry 'from TV's *Frenton High*'. Furious negotiation between the two actors' agents and the theatre management had led to them being given exactly equal billing, in terms of font and photograph size. But Tilly Marcus, whose name appeared on the left-hand side of the poster and would therefore be first to catch the eye, might feel that she had gained a tiny advantage over her soap-star rival.

The actor playing the other Ugly Sister, Dyspepsia, was called Danny Fitz and he was way down the poster, both in position and font size. The fact that he was one of the most experienced and brilliant pantomime dames in the country went for nothing – he didn't have any television credits.

The show's Buttons was to be Felix Fisher, who had plenty of TV panel shows to list after his name. He had started out as a very gay foul-mouthed stand-up, wearing flamboyant costumes and heavy make-up, and was now negotiating the difficult passage towards lovability and hopefully hosting a television game-show. The theory was that Buttons, the cheery kitchen boy of whose adoration Cinderella is unaware, would be a perfect stepping stone on that journey. And no one in the produc-tion company putting on *Cinderella* seemed to have seen anything incongruous in casting in the role someone whose shtick was his gayness. Maybe the thinking was that the kiddies in the audience would not find anything odd in his avowals of love for Cinderella, and the older members would find humour in its irony.

Certainly nobody involved in the production seemed to have thought that changing round the casting of Tad Gentry and Felix Fisher might have been a good idea, thus achieving a straight Buttons and another camp Ugly Sister. But no, the thinking had not gone that far. All the production company wanted was names with television credits to put on the poster.

Charles Paris was amazed that they'd even found a couple to put by his name. Neither series had been much of a success, and both had been an extremely long time ago, but sure enough under his name was the byline 'from TV's *The Strutters* and *Stanislas*

Braid'. Mind you, in the lowly role of one of the Broker's Men, he didn't justify a photograph.

His fellow Broker's Man, however, did. In the bizarre manner of celebrity casting for pantomimes, the part had been given to an ex-boxer. A promising light-welterweight as an amateur, Mick 'The Cobra' Mesquito had turned professional at the age of nineteen. Having moved up to the welterweight division and defeated most domestic opposition, he had had one shot at a world title, when he'd been humiliatingly thrashed by a Puerto Rican. He continued fighting against ever less distinguished opposition until a detached retina caused him to hang up his gloves.

It was then that a pushy management company decided to promote the media career of Mick 'The Cobra' Mesquito. He was initially put forward as a pundit on boxing coverage, but they had ambitions for him to go further. He was good-looking and the genes from his Caribbean father had given him a colour that was very attractive to television companies in search of diversity. The fact that he was no good at any of the presenting roles he'd been given had not so far impeded the progress of his new career.

Whether Mick 'The Cobra' Mesquito was any good at pantomime remained to be seen. But his fellow Broker's Man Charles Paris was not overly optimistic.

Kenny Polizzi was remarkably affable at rehearsals. He didn't play the big star. He didn't seem worried that, in spite of his top billing, Baron Hardup was a relatively small part in the Cinderella story. Maybe he thought he'd achieved enough not to have anything to prove.

And when he was introduced to his fellow cast members, his modest charm was maintained. He twinkled for the girls, and was bonhomous to the boys. There was only one moment of slight awkwardness when he was introduced to Tad Gentry ('from TV's *Frenton High*'). The younger actor gave the star a huge bear-hug and said, 'Great to see you again, Kenny.'

This prompted a look of puzzlement. 'Have we met before?'

'Yes. In LA. At the premiere of that Julia Roberts movie.'

Kenny shook his head. 'Sorry, don't recall it.'

The disruption was a very minor one. Kenny had been perfectly courteous, but the peevish expression on Tad's face showed he felt he'd been the victim of a major public snub.

Kenny's lack of starriness did not mean, however, that there were no conflicts at rehearsal. Though the imported big name was behaving himself, there were plenty of others in the company who were capable of making trouble.

The two soap stars, for a start, didn't see eye to eye. Tilly Marcus reckoned that because she was still currently in *Gatley Road*, this gave her automatic superiority over Tad Gentry, whose regular role as sexy villain in *Frenton High* had been curtailed by a spectacular fictional motorbike crash some three years previously. Also, Tilly was playing the name part in *Cinderella*, which by her reckoning meant she was the show's real star. And being the star gave her automatic full flouncing rights.

Nor was there much warmth between Tad and his fellow Ugly Sister. A large man whose bulky body tapered down to very tiny feet, Danny Fitz was a legend amongst *aficionados* of pantomime. His dame was mentioned in the same breath as those giants of the role, Dan Leno, Nat Jackley, Arthur Askey, Billy Dainty and Jack Tripp. But such names meant little to the contemporary television-obsessed world.

Nor did the traditional pantomime routines over which Danny Fitz had such mastery. Previously, whenever he'd done *Cinderella*, his fellow Ugly Sister had been a comic actor called Bobby Crowther. Though both had been gay, their partnership had never been anything but professional. In fact they hadn't even liked each other very much, but the magic they created together on stage was hailed by audiences and critics alike. With Bobby's death the previous year, this was the first time Danny was doing the Ugly Sisters without him.

And Tad was not proving the ideal substitute. Like many soap stars, he couldn't actually act . . . or perhaps it would be more accurate to say he could only act one part and that was himself. Which was fine and indeed simplified the process of the soap-opera production line whereby endless indistinguishable scenes were being recorded at great speed, but it didn't help a lot when Tad was playing an Ugly Sister.

He made no attempt even to change his voice. Each time

Danny suggested that he might try a bit of falsetto, Tad would say, 'No, if I do that, my fans won't know it's me.'

'But they'll be able to see it's you.'

'No, I'm not putting on a funny voice.'

'It's not a funny voice,' said Danny, his large body looming over Tad. 'It's a voice that's right for the character.'

'No, that's not the way I work.'

This kind of disagreement could have been sorted out by a strong director, but Bix Rogers didn't fit that job description. Showing his background as a choreographer, the only bits of *Cinderella* that really interested him were the musical numbers. He lavished rehearsal time and attention on those and basically reckoned the actors could work out the dialogue scenes on their own.

This behaviour was not as unusual in pantomime as it might have been in other areas of theatrical performance. Pantomime scripts had always been rather fluid, passed on year by year. Charles Paris remembered being in an *Aladdin* in which the gap between two songs was simply marked 'Trombone Biz'. It turned out that the previous year's Abanazar had been an elderly comic whose speciality was a routine with a trombone, which had been duly shoehorned into the story. The year Charles was in it, the Abanazar was an elderly comic whose shtick was making animals out of balloons. No doubt, the gap between the two songs in the following year's script read 'Balloon Biz'.

Pantomime songs also frequently had very little relevance to the story that was being told. In the days of music hall, comedians in pantomimes would simply insert the songs that were a regular part of their act. And in the age of pop stars a slot was usually found, for the character's latest single. While the number was belted out, the plot would simply be put on hold.

The situation wasn't quite that bad in the Empire Theatre Eastbourne's *Cinderella*. There was a basic script and there was even reputed to be a writer. Certainly someone must have created the routine in which Kenny Polizzi used all of his *Dwight House* catchphrases. And the songs, though not original, had been standards chosen more or less to fit in with the mood at various points in the storyline.

The exception to this of course was the song that Cinderella sang when left alone in the kitchen after her father and the Ugly Sisters had gone off to Prince Charming's ball. Normally for this moment a wistful ballad of loneliness is selected, but the Empire Theatre production was scheduled to feature the single from Tilly Marcus's first album, which had only recently been released. Called 'Dance With Your Body', its connection to the *Cinderella* story was tenuous to say the least, but it did give Bix Rogers a wonderful opportunity to choreograph a big number with a chorus of rats, mice, kettles and saucepans.

At the afternoon tea break of that Wednesday's rehearsal Danny Fitz was clearly still very upset about having to work with Tad Gentry. He slumped wearily into a seat next to Charles. 'God, what I thought was going to be my dream job is clearly going to be a nightmare from start to finish.'

'Why was it so much your dream job?' asked Charles.

'Well, I always love doing the Sisters. They're different from other dames, because most of those are basically benign characters. But no, the Ugly Sisters are pure evil. Oh, they may get forgiven at the end of the story and they may have lines during the Walkdown where they say they're going to reform, but don't believe a word of it. They're at least as bad as Regan and Goneril – to whom of course they bear an uncanny resemblance . . . you know, if you think of King Lear as Baron Hardup, the Fool as Buttons, Edmund as the Demon King – oh, *King Lear* really works as a panto. But that's by the by.'

'So it's because you like playing an evil character that this is your dream job?'

'Well, partly that, but also geography.'

'Sorry?'

'I actually live here in Eastbourne.'

'Oh, do you?'

'Yes, I run a very neat little B&B, you know, to keep the pennies coming in when the National Theatre fails to ring yet again. I really just do the pantos these days. Used to do summer season as well, but that's dead in the water now. They don't want variety bills any more. Why bother? Much cheaper to set up a tour for some foul-mouthed comedian off the telly, have him effing and blinding round all the number-one venues. Yes, so it's

great for me that this show's in Eastbourne. Not so great that
I've been paired up with Tad Gentry. I've seen planks of wood
with more acting talent than he's got.'

'But presumably you knew this was going to be difficult – the
first year you've done the Ugly Sisters without Bobby Crowther.'

'Maybe, but surely they could have cast someone with some
instinct for panto. I mean I know any number of old actors who
could be brought out of retirement and do better than Tad. He's
just destroying everything I've worked for all these years. He
and Kenny Polizzi are ruining what I'm trying to do. God, I'd
like to kill the bloody pair of them!' Danny concluded with
petulant bitterness.

In spite of the level of textual embroidery going on elsewhere
in the show, Charles Paris, as one of the Broker's Men, tended
to stick to the script as written. This was partly because Mick
'The Cobra' Mesquito, whose hold on the lines was never going
to be strong, might be thrown by any changes in his cues, but
also because Charles wasn't that keen on improvisation. His
distaste for it dated back to a long three months he'd spent with
one of those directors who say their scripts are 'created in the
mutual white heat of improvisation with their ensemble', and
then claim for themselves all the royalties for the published text
and subsequent productions.

The play that emerged was too long (as improvised shows
always are) and would have been better with a writer giving
some shape to it (as improvised shows always would). It was
set on a failing family farm in Devon and Charles had bleached
all recollection of it out of his mind. All recollection that is
except for the review he got from the *Hampstead and Highgate
Express*. 'It was hard to tell whether Charles Paris's curled nostril
was a response to the farmyard smells or to the script.'

Because of Bix Rogers' background as a choreographer, the
Eastbourne *Cinderella* featured more dancers than many pantomimes. And they were professional dancers, not children from
the local ballet school (which had proved a cheap way of filling
out the cast list of many a pantomime). The casting of adults
was partly because of Bix's choreographic ambitions, but also
because new rules about the chaperoning and protection of

under-age performers in a theatre made booking them more trouble than it was worth.

Charles had been in shows with dancers before. Indeed the Jacqui with whom he'd such a rewarding time in Worthing had been primarily a dancer. And he was always struck by how different they were from actors. Their priorities obviously included physical fitness and a mechanistic discipline. And though they were outgoing and friendly to the rest of the company, socially they tended to stick together.

They also talked in a choreographic shorthand which was hard for a non-dancer to understand. For example, there was usually one dancer called the 'swing'. He or she was a kind of universal understudy, knowing everyone's choreography and able to step into the shoes of any dancer who was sick or injured. Then there was the 'dance captain', a member of the chorus line who during the run of a show acted as the choreographer's representative. The dance captain led the warm-ups before performances and generally ensured that the choreography kept up to the standard with which it had started the run.

In the Empire Theatre's *Cinderella* this role was taken by a dancer called Jasmine del Rio, who was as likely to have been born with that name as she was with her ash-blonde hair. Like most dancers Jasmine had a fabulously slender body and looked wonderfully glamorous on stage. Seen closer to, the effect was less stunning. In spite of heavy make-up, her face had that papier mâché skin quality which marks out a heavy smoker. (Charles was constantly amazed by how much dancers smoked. For them fitness was clearly a relative term.)

Because of Bix Rogers' background, the chorus line for *Cinderella* was bigger than it would be for most pantomimes, where savage cost-cutting and cast reduction were primary concerns. (Charles remembered being told by a fellow actor of one particular cheapskate production of *Ali Baba and the Forty Thieves* which contained the line: 'You come with me. You thirty-nine wait out there.')

And Bix Rogers' chorus line, following the *de rigueur* trend of all West End musicals, had a multi-ethnic composition. Although, except for Jasmine del Rio's mid-Atlantic twang, most of the accents derived from Essex or Liverpool, many of the dancers' forbears had African or Asian origins. There was one particularly gorgeous Chinese – or perhaps half-Chinese – girl called Kitty Woo who Charles had difficulty in tearing his eyes away from during rehearsal. Supple of body and golden of skin, her image of oriental exotica was only let down by the cockney rasp which emerged every time she opened her mouth.

Kitty seemed to be a particular friend of Jasmine del Rio. The two of them bustled off together out of the St Asaph's Church Halls whenever there was a break, instantly picking up an uninterrupted flow of gossip and fags.

A recurrent factor in rehearsals for all the pantomimes Charles Paris had been involved in was that there simply weren't enough of them. The Eastbourne *Cinderella* was not unusual in having less than two weeks to get the show together. The result of this would be that the first week's performances (two a day, afternoon and evening) would really be a work in progress, a continuation of rehearsal witnessed by paying audiences. By the second week of the run the cast would have settled into their proper routine, though the amount of ad-libbing the comics indulged in meant that no two performances were ever the same.

Kenny Polizzi seemed to have attached himself to Charles Paris, a situation to which Charles had no objection at all. At the end of his first day's rehearsal, Kenny said, 'Time for a quick one?', and they ended up in the Sea Dog, where they had first met. It was the nearest pub to the St Asaph's Church Halls and aspired to Victorian cosiness. There was a lot of coloured glass in the decor, stuffed birds in glass cases and monochrome photos of old Eastbourne on the walls. In the hearth a log fire blazed, and you had to look at it for a long time till you realized that the logs weren't being consumed by the hissing gas.

When it came to liquor, Charles was amazed at Kenny's restraint. In the unlikely event of Charles himself ever giving up the booze, the last place he'd want to socialize in would be a pub. Too much temptation all around. The very smell of the place would be a challenge to his resolve.

But Kenny Polizzi liked the atmosphere of what he called 'a genuine English pub'. Meekly ordering mineral water, he showed no signs of discomfort in the environment. Maybe he regarded these visits as some kind of challenge, proving to himself how complete was his victory over the demon drink.

They were in the pub after Wednesday's rehearsal, Charles restoring the tissues with a large Bell's, Kenny with his eternal mineral water, when they were joined by someone Charles hadn't met.

The newcomer was a rubber ball of a man who moved across the bar with great urgency. It soon became apparent that he did everything with great urgency. He wore a grey suit, tight and crumpled as though he had slept in it. His bald dome was inadequately covered by an untidy comb-over which he kept unconsciously trying to flatten with his right hand.

'Lefty!' cried Kenny Polizzi, rising to envelop him in a man-hug. 'Lefty, I'd like you to meet Charles Paris. He's acting in *Cinderella* too. Charles – Lefty Rubenstein. Lefty's my agent.'

'"Agent" don't cover it,' said Lefty, sitting down at the table. His accent was Californian, but not the laid-back kind. He sounded busy, urgent. 'For "agent" read "minder", "fixer", "gopher" and "nursemaid".'

'Don't forget also, Lefty, that you source all the stuff I need.'

There was clearly more significance in that line than might appear. Lefty Rubenstein nodded vigorously and said, 'Yeah, yeah, I got what you asked me to get you.'

Kenny spread his hands wide. 'Hey, isn't this great? One of the few advantages to being a star. You get a Lefty Rubenstein to organize everything for you. All good news for everyone.'

'Not for everyone,' the agent grumbled. 'Certainly not if you happen to *be* Lefty Rubenstein.'

His boss grinned. Clearly this kind of badinage was part of some long-established double act between them. 'It's true, though, Charles,' he said, 'Lefty runs my life – but don't start feeling sorry for him because he gets very well paid for doing so.'

'You think any amount of money could begin to compensate for the aggravation you put me through?'

'Can it, Lefty. You love the job.'

'Oh yeah? Only one hundred per cent wrong there, Kenny. I hate the job. You never understand this. Not love. Hate!'

'Lefty, you are just so full of shit.'

'You're fuller of shit than I am any day.'

The two Americans were clearly enjoying insulting each other, so Charles Paris asked if he could get Lefty a drink.

'Diet Coke, please.' He looked across at Kenny Polizzi's mineral water. 'You got a gin or vodka in that?'

'Nothing. I'm officially off the booze – period.'

'Huh,' Lefty snorted. 'I heard that one before.'

'This time it's for good.'

Another 'Huh.' Then he called out to Charles, who had just got up on his way to the bar, 'Just don't be around when he falls off the wagon.'

'I'm not going to fall off the wagon,' Charles heard Kenny protest. 'I've found out where and when the AA meets right here in Eastbourne'

When he rejoined them with the Diet Coke, Charles was treated to a lot more about Lefty Rubenstein. He was one of those people who felt he had to give a complete résumé to everyone he met. Having told Charles he had just arrived from Los Angeles that day, he then went a long way back into his personal history. The 'Lefty' nickname came from when he had been a devious pitcher at college baseball . . . though the idea of his roly-poly figure ever having played any sport was now totally incongruous.

He'd trained as a lawyer and it was in that capacity that he first met Kenny Polizzi. But he had found he was spending so much of his time arguing the details of his client's professional contracts that he might as well ace out the existing agent and take on the role himself. From that time he had handled all of Kenny's business and personal affairs. 'And let me tell you, dealing with all those sharks in the television industry is a breeze along the boardwalk compared to the personal stuff. Jesus, all those ex-wives.'

'They were perfectly nice women when I married them,' Kenny contributed, in a pose of bewildered innocence.

'Yeah, well, something happened when you wanted to unmarry them. They all turned into monsters.'

'That's true, Lefty. Strange – who'da thought living with me would have that effect?'

'Anyone who'd spent five minutes in your company, Kenny.'

'Oh hey, that's a bit harsh.'

'Harsh, but true.' The agent appealed to Charles. 'Before I

met this bastard I had hair to comb over my comb-over. Look at it now.' So at least he had a sense of humour about his coiffure.

'Dare I ask,' said Kenny, 'whether you've heard any more communication with the Plague from Palm Springs?'

'Yes.'

'And?'

'And she's still mad as hell at you.'

'I know that, Lefty. But are she and her posse of lawyers any closer to signing the agreements?'

The lawyer shook his hands from side to side in an equivocating manner. 'They're still playing edgy with that. One day they're about to sign the whole thing off, next day something's come up.' He turned to Charles to elucidate. 'The lady we're discussing—'

'Who certainly doesn't qualify for the title of "lady",' said Kenny.

'. . . is the most recent Mrs Polizzi. Indeed, until she signs on the dotted line, she is the *current* Mrs Polizzi.'

'She was mentioned on *The Johnny Martin Show*,' said Charles.

'Sure she was. Lilith Greenstone.'

'Easy to recognize,' said Kenny. 'Ten per cent sugar candy, ninety per cent vitriol. Hey, you've never said, Charlie boy . . . are you married?'

'Erm . . . I'm not unmarried.' It was the nearest he could come to defining his on/off relationship with Frances.

But fortunately Kenny wasn't really interested in further details. He was still absorbed in his ongoing sparring match with his agent. 'So what did the fragrant Lilith say when she last communicated with you, Lefty?'

'Well, needless to say, she didn't communicate with me direct. Everything comes through her lawyers. You know . . .' Lefty's tone became sentimental '. . . a lot of nasty things are said about lawyers. All those unkind jokes comparing the profession to various predators. You know, like "Why won't sharks eat lawyers? Professional courtesy." I don't like to hear lawyers being described like that . . . but for Lilith Greenstone's lawyers I'll make an exception!' he concluded viciously.

'Come on, though – what did she say?'

'She said you were the worst kind of skunk, to run away to England.'

'Hey, I haven't "run away to England",' protested Kenny, mock-aggrieved. 'I've come over here to work. I'm extending my range by taking on the onerous role of Baron Hardup in a very fine production of *Cinderella*.'

'Well, you can tell Lilith that when she arrives.'

'"When she arrives"? Hell, is she planning to come over here?'

'I think she's bluffing, but that's what she said. She said she thought you two might have to meet face to face.'

'She wants to sort out the final details of the divorce?'

'No, I think she just wants to sort you out.'

'Oh.' Kenny's expression suggested that encounter was not one he would enjoy.

And so the double act went on. Charles was content just to sit and listen. Though he was quite capable of being the life and soul of any party, it was just an act (like most things in his life, he thought in his less cheerful moments). But he was also happy to be entertained by the conversation of others.

They had another round of drinks – large Bell's for Charles, mineral water for Kenny, Diet Coke for Lefty. (Charles was to discover that the agent was almost never seen without a bottle of Diet Coke in his hand – he seemed to need an intravenous drip of the stuff.) Then Kenny said he should take Lefty to his hotel – the agent's bags had been delivered there, but he hadn't checked in yet.

'Are you in the Grand, like me?'

'Hell, no. The *Cinderella* production company's picking up your tab. My company, using my money, has opted for somewhere slightly less grand.'

'I'll walk you round there.'

The two Americans went out of the pub together, but Charles needed a pee. Having not been since lunchtime, he'd needed one when he first arrived in the pub, but not for the first time alcohol had diverted his intentions. By now, with two double Bell's inside him, the need was quite urgent.

He crossed the bar from the Gents, giving a half-hearted wave to the barmaid, who didn't notice the gesture. He was about to leave when something he saw through the bubbled glass of the window made him stop.

It had come on to rain and the seafront of Eastbourne looked particularly drab and Novemberish. Protected from the rain by the awning over the pub's door stood Kenny Polizzi and his agent.

Lefty was giving something to his boss.

It was a semi-automatic pistol.

Within seconds it was hidden in Kenny's coat pocket and the two men were walking away.

THREE

FIRST BROKER'S MAN: I've just read a book about three
   holes in the ground.
SECOND BROKER'S MAN: Well, well, well.
FIRST BROKER'S MAN: Yes, that was the title.

C harles picked up a tuna sandwich from a convenience
store on his way back to his digs. The accommodation,
recommended by the Empire Theatre, had been described
as 'self-catering', but Charles wasn't much of a one for cooking.
He rarely aspired beyond a tin of baked beans on toast. That
evening a tuna sandwich would do him fine . . . so long as he'd
got a bottle of Bell's by way of accompaniment. And he was
confident there was one back at the digs.

In spite of the rain through which he splashed, the front at
Eastbourne still retained the Victorian elegance which had once
seen it called 'the Empress of Watering Places'. Lights still shone
from the pier, with its blue and white paint, its Victorian Tea
Rooms, its Atlantis night club at the end. Charles loved the tacky
charm of English seaside towns out of season.

He felt sure he'd come to Eastbourne with his wife Frances
when their daughter Juliet was tiny. Hadn't they travelled on the
trackless Dotto train with her along the seafront? Or was that in
Hastings? Whichever, it had been a good memory. Mixing an
actor's life and marriage had seemed very simple then. That
reminded him – he must ring Frances.

By the entrance to the pier he turned away from the front,
towards the shabbier hinterland of the town where his digs were.
And as he did so, Charles thought about the scene he had just
witnessed outside the Sea Dog. He felt pretty sure that the handover
of the pistol followed on from what Lefty had said to Kenny, 'I
got what you asked me to get you.'

Charles also remembered Kenny saying on *The Johnny Martin
Show* that he felt naked without a gun. Maybe there was more

to it than that. Maybe, as someone with such a high public profile, Kenny Polizzi was genuinely worried about crackpots and stalkers and carried a gun for self-protection.

Charles concluded that there probably wasn't anything sinister about what he had just witnessed. And it wasn't his business, anyway. But he couldn't completely clear his mind of the memory.

The tuna sandwich he found when he got to his digs wasn't very nice. Though the label carried that day's date, it tasted like it had spent rather longer on the refrigerated shelf than it should have done. It had certainly had time to get very soggy. Hard to tell where the brown bread stopped and the tuna started.

Perhaps he should have stayed in the Sea Dog after Kenny and Lefty went, ordered something to eat there. It was a decision Charles had to make quite often in his life. Though some of his meals were boozy, boisterous affairs with other actors, his chosen lifestyle meant that he usually ate on his own. Over the years he'd had a lot of sad sandwiches and melancholy microwaving in his Hereford Road flat or in anonymous digs all over the country.

Of the bleak alternatives, he actually preferred eating alone in a pub, with only the *Times* crossword for company. Being with other people – even other people he didn't know or talk to – was better than being contained within the all too familiar parameters of what he rarely called 'home'. But he couldn't do it too often. Even lowly pub food was getting increasingly expensive, and he wasn't being paid that much as a Broker's Man.

In his capacity as a Broker's Man it had been a bad day's rehearsal. The Broker's Men don't have a lot to do in *Cinderella*. Indeed in many pantomime versions they don't even figure. But in the Empire Theatre version they were involved in all the big scenes and had a few moments to themselves. The biggest was near the beginning of the show, when they appeared at Baron Hardup's shabby castle, threatening to turn him and his daughters out on to the street for non-payment of rent.

But since this scene also involved the first entrance of Baron Hardup, Charles' and Mick 'The Cobra' Mesquito's parts had been severely truncated. By the time Kenny had come on, done his routine about Dwight Bredon with all his catchphrases from *The Dwight House* and sung the show's signature tune, there

wasn't much time left for the Broker's Men. Or for much of
Cinderella's plot, come to that.

In some ways this was a relief to Charles. Though no actor
likes having his lines cut, having to be on the stage for less time
with Mick 'The Cobra' Mesquito was a definite bonus. Charles
had worked with quite a few actors who weren't very good, but
never with one who had as little sense of the theatre as Mick
Mesquito. Maybe it was a legacy of the cauliflower ears he had
received from boxing, but he certainly had a tin ear for dialogue.

To Charles, having been an actor so long, intonation and
emphasis were second nature. He also had an instinctive sense
of the rhythm of a line.

Mick 'The Cobra' Mesquito lacked all of these qualities –
particularly the sense of rhythm. Which mattered more in the
Empire Theatre's *Cinderella* than it might in other shows because
most of the script was written in rhyming couplets. Which Mick
Mesquito drove through like a bulldozer.

For example, take a simple exchange like . . .

*FIRST BROKER'S MAN: If you don't give your castle yard
up . . .*

SECOND BROKER'S MAN: We will make you, Baron Hardup.

It doesn't sound so good if the second speaker ignores the punc-
tuation and makes his line sound like a dire threat of infertility.
'We will make you barren, Hardup.'

But that was the kind of thing that came up constantly in
rehearsal. If a line could be mangled, then Mick 'The Cobra'
Mesquito would mangle it. Charles tried very gently to push
him in the direction of the right intonation, but to no avail.
The former boxer wasn't offended by these attempts to help;
he just clearly couldn't hear the difference between the way
Charles said the lines and the way he did. And, needless to
say, their director Bix Rogers was far too busy staging another
massive musical number to devote any attention to the spoken
bits of the script.

So Charles didn't reckon being half of a double act with Mick
'The Cobra' Mesquito was going to be the most fulfilling role
of his theatrical career. It reminded him of being part of another
pairing in *Hamlet* at Hornchurch. And of the review that that
performance elicited. 'Charles Paris seemed unsure as to whether

he was Rosencrantz or Guildenstern and, quite honestly, the way he played the part, who cared?' *Romford Recorder*.

After finishing his soggy sandwich, Charles poured himself a large measure of Bell's. He'd have liked some ice in it, but although his self-catering digs did boast a fridge, he had omitted to refill the ice tray. He would have liked to settle down to the *Times* crossword, but there had been sufficient longueurs for him to have completed it at rehearsal.

The digs boasted a television too, but a quick zap through the available channels told him that there was nothing he wanted to watch. That seemed to happen increasingly. Particularly with drama. The effort of engaging his interest in a new set of characters was becoming more and more difficult. Was that just a sign of age? Or was it the old thing of feeling jealous of actors who'd got lucrative television work when he hadn't?

He looked at the pile of books by his bedside, but nothing appealed. Charles was one of those people who'd always got a book on the go, but the last couple of weeks he'd started a few without finding one that commanded his attention. He found that was often the case when he began rehearsing something. Even when he was only playing a humble Broker's Man, he found it difficult to focus on anything apart from the show.

He remembered the thought he'd had walking back along the front. He could ring Frances. They were still married, after all, though the last time they'd spoken she'd sounded more distant than ever. Charles knew his track record as a husband wasn't great. Young actresses were an occupational hazard of his profession, but it was a while now since he had even the mildest skirmish with anyone of the opposite sex. That made him feel almost virtuous.

At times he wondered whether he really was past all that. The mornings he woke up alone with an arid hangover it seemed impossible to imagine that bed had ever been a place of such all-consuming pleasure. And he was getting older too. Maybe his libido was just fading away like the pain from an old injury.

He'd have that thought for days, sometimes even weeks. Yes, it was all over. Charles Paris had made love for the last time. The thought made him walk around in numb despair.

But then when he was on the tube he'd catch the swirl of a skirt or the wobble of a bottom . . . or he'd find himself after rehearsal chatting to some extraordinarily well-constructed assistant stage manager . . . and lust came surging back like a rainstorm in the desert, carrying all before it and enabling all kinds of hopes and fantasies to spring up in its wake. And he knew it wasn't all quite over yet.

He still felt lust for Frances too, but that was more complicated. He'd let her down so many times. There had been many rapprochements and many heartfelt vows from Charles to mend his ways. And he always meant what he said when he said it, when he was with Frances. But somehow when he was somewhere else, when he was with someone else . . . the vows he'd made didn't seem so important.

He thought the chances of his ever re-establishing a permanent position in Frances's bed were remote.

Still, he did want to ring her that evening. He needed to talk to her. He still loved her, after all. In a way. Ernest Dowson's most famous line came unbidden into his head. '*I have been faithful to thee, Cynara, in my fashion.*' But he feared it wasn't a definition of 'faithful' that Frances would accept.

He was fairly confident, though, that she still felt something for him. But not confident enough to ask her to define what that something was.

The phone rang for a long time. He was about to ring off when Frances answered. She sounded very tired. Of course, Charles reminded himself, getting towards the end of the autumn term. Everything that needed to be sorted out running up to Christmas. Always tough for a headmistress. (It was strange, Charles never thought about it at any other time, but the minute he got back in touch with Frances, he reminded himself how the rhythm of her year was dictated by school terms and holidays.)

'Hi, it's Charles.'

'Oh. To what do I owe this rare pleasure?'

'Well, I just thought . . . we haven't been in touch for a while.'

'That is certainly true.' Was Charles imagining it or did he actually hear his wife stifling a yawn?

'So I'm making up for lost time.'

'I sometimes think, Charles, that you have already lost so

much time, there isn't enough time left in the world for you to make it up.'

He was rather afraid that what she'd said wasn't a joke, but he laughed at it all the same.

'Anyway, Frances, how are you?'

There was a slight pause before she said, 'Fine.'

'Good.'

'And you?'

'Not so bad.'

'Working?'

'Yes, I actually am . . . so there's a novelty.'

'Doing what?'

'Well, I'm in this . . . Surely I told you?'

'You haven't been in touch for three months, Charles.'

'Three months? I can't believe it's as long as—'

'Three months,' Frances confirmed in a manner that excluded further argument. 'So what is it you're doing?'

Charles gave a quick summary of how he ended up playing a Broker's Man in *Cinderella* at the Empire Theatre Eastbourne. 'And the star – well, the guy who's playing Baron Hardup – is none other than Kenny Polizzi.'

'Name's vaguely familiar. Remind me.'

'Star of *The Dwight House*.'

'I've heard of the show, don't think I've ever seen it.'

Charles reminded himself that Frances had never watched much television. Too busy marking most evenings. And when she did watch something, it tended to be serious documentaries or drama. She'd never shared his taste for crap television.

'Well, take my word for it – he's a big name.'

'Ah.' Once again Frances sounded impossibly weary.

'Are you all right?'

'Yes. I hope so.'

'What do you mean by that?'

'Oh, it's probably nothing.'

'You can't say that, Frances.'

'What do you mean?'

'Well, you can't just leave things in the air. "Oh, it's probably nothing" is about the most worrying thing anyone can say to anyone. It opens out too many possibilities. What's the matter? Are you ill?'

'I hope not.'

'What does that mean?'

Frances sighed a long, weary sigh. 'I had to go to the hospital last week for some tests.'

'Tests for what?'

'I've got a lump.'

'A lump on your breast?'

'Yes. As I say, it's probably nothing. But they took a biopsy at the hospital and it's being checked out, and I'm sure I'll find out it's nothing.'

Charles felt terrible, as if everything solid in his life was suddenly crumbling away. 'Frances, does anyone else know about this?'

'Of course. I've told most of my friends. If it is breast cancer, then it's good to have a network of support. And don't worry, it's a very curable disease these days.'

'Does Juliet know?'

'Of course she does.'

'And Miles?'

'Yes.'

That seemed to hurt even more. The thought that his loathed son-in-law, the one who had the temerity to call him 'Pop', knew about the situation while he didn't was extraordinarily painful.

He couldn't put off the question any longer. 'Why didn't you tell me, Frances?'

She sighed again. 'Because, Charles, there didn't seem any point in worrying you unnecessarily. I'm doing quite enough worrying for both of us.'

'But I am your husband.'

'No longer a very good argument, Charles.'

'But—'

'I was going to ring you after I'd got the results of the biopsy.'

'When will that be?'

'They said it'd be about a week, so . . . Friday with a following wind. May take longer. You never know.'

'I'll definitely ring you Friday,' said Charles. 'When I get a break in rehearsal. Promise I'll do that.'

'OK,' said the tired voice. 'And then hopefully I'll just be able to tell you that everything is fine.'

'Yes.' He was silent for a moment, then couldn't help asking, 'But, Frances, why didn't you tell me before?'

'What would have been the point, Charles?'

'But it makes me feel like I'm not part of your life.'

'If you're not, whose fault is that?' He couldn't supply an answer. 'I'd have told you if you'd rung me, Charles.'

FOUR

NAUSEA: My sister and I are fastidious.
DYSPEPSIA: Yes, I'm fast and she's hideous.

Charles Paris was preoccupied during the following day's rehearsals. Nobody noticed anything different about him – he was normally one of the quieter members of the company – but his mind kept turning back to thoughts of Frances. He wasn't by nature good at finding out positive scenarios, and had a tendency to think the worst. The worst he could think about Frances's situation was pretty grim. The thought of the threat to her, the idea that she might not always be in his life, hurt like physical pain. And he could not lose the feeling that he was somehow to blame for what was happening to her.

The Broker's Men were not involved much in the day's rehearsals, but Charles stayed around St Asaph's Church Halls. He didn't want to be on his own with his worries. Bix Rogers was off in the main hall, elaborating the choreography for Tilly Marcus's 'Dance With Your Body' routine, and in the smaller hall the Ugly Sisters, Baron Hardup and Buttons were rehearsing their kitchen slapstick scene (which preceded Dandini's arrival with invitations to Prince Charming's ball).

This was another area of the pantomime where virtually no script existed, but Danny Fitz had taken charge, trying to coach his fellow actors into a routine that might well have been a hundred years old. There was a lot of water, flour and dough involved, so it was one of those scenes for which a protective sheet had to be ceremoniously laid down on the stage.

The participants were meant to be making a cake and Buttons kept being sent off to fetch the necessary components – or rather to fetch the wrong components. Thus, when ordered by Nausea and Dyspepsia to fetch the 'ingredients', he came back with a jar full of 'greedy ants'. And when asked to bring 'flour', he returned with a single rose, prompting the following exchange:

NAUSEA: What's that?
BUTTONS: You said get a little flower. So I got one.
NAUSEA: Not that kind of flower. What sort is it anyway?
BUTTONS: It's a chrysanthemum.
NAUSEA: No, it's not, it's a rose.
BUTTONS: It's a chrysanthemum.
NAUSEA: It's a rose.
BUTTONS: It's a chrysanthemum.
NAUSEA: All right. Spell chrysanthemum.
BUTTONS: Errrr . . . It's a rose.

Danny Fitz had an amazing memory for such sequences of crosstalk. He had been playing dames for over thirty years and was like a walking encyclopedia of the genre. The trouble was, though, that he had such respect for the ancient pantomime routines that he didn't like to see a single detail of them changed.

Which had been fine when he had been working with Bobby Crowther, who had been as well drilled in the tradition as Danny himself. But Bobby was dead and it wasn't going so well trying to recreate the scenes with Kenny Polizzi, Tad Gentry and Felix Fisher. None of them could see why they should stick to the script that Danny remembered so exactly. And each of them thought they could make the routine funnier by adding jokes of their own.

This was a particular problem with Buttons. With his background in outrageous stand-up, Felix had a lot of experience in holding an audience's attention and in ad-libbing. But he had very little experience of working with other actors. Stand-ups are rarely team players. So he didn't like having the creaky structure of an old-fashioned slapstick routine imposed on him. And he reckoned he could come up with better lines than the ones that Danny was trying to make him say.

And although Buttons was meant to be a step on the way to becoming a family-friendly performer, Felix's stand-up training told him he could always get a laugh by being crude.

For example, Danny was trying to get him to say the following lines:

> BUTTONS: *How can I tell when this cake's cooked?*
> NAUSEA: *You stick a knife in it and if it comes out clean,*
>   *it's cooked.*
> BUTTONS: *Oh, good, if it comes out clean I'll stick all the*
>   *other dirty knives in it too.*

Not great, but traditional and it might well get a laugh based on the enduring stupidity of Buttons' character.

Felix, however, thought it would be funnier if he were to make his second line, 'Oh, good, I'll stick my dick in too – that could do with a clean-up, after the unlikely places it's been.'

Charles didn't say anything but he felt sympathy for Danny trying to explain to the stand-up that the line a) wasn't funny, b) didn't fit into the pantomime tradition, and c) would be totally unsuitable for a matinee full of pre-teens.

The wrangling went on for some time. Kenny retained his customary cool and didn't take sides, but Tad was with Felix all the way. Watching from the sidelines, Charles felt acutely embarrassed, particularly when Felix started telling Danny that he ought to 'come into the twenty-first century'. Audiences, he said, 'don't mind a bit of smut these days – in fact, they feel cheated if they don't get it.'

Danny countered that *double entendres* were fine, indeed the stock-in-trade of many pantomime routines, but there was no ambiguity in the lines that Felix was coming up with. They could only be interpreted one way – and that was as filth.

'Look,' said Felix, his false lashes flickering dangerously under their glittering eyeliner, 'I can guarantee you that that line will get a laugh.'

'Possibly,' came the waspish reply from Danny. 'You could flash your willy at the audience and that'd probably get a laugh too. But it wouldn't be the right kind of laugh.'

Charles was deeply aware of how much time was being wasted by this argument. The rehearsal schedule was already tight enough without battling over the script. Though Bix was polishing up the musical numbers to a high professional gloss, there were whole dialogue scenes that still hadn't even been looked at. It was Thursday and the show was opening on the following Friday.

Eventually Kenny said something. His stance as a neutral didn't stop him from being aware of the waste of rehearsal time. 'Hey, guys,' he began in a conciliatory tone, 'let's not get this out of proportion. I think I see a solution here.'

'The solution,' said Danny, 'is to do the traditional kitchen slapstick scene.'

'Not necessarily. All that's needed is a funny scene, something for the audience to laugh at.'

'And they will laugh at the traditional kitchen slapstick scene – if it's done right.'

'Sure,' Kenny agreed. 'But it might be easier to do something completely different.'

'Completely different – like what?'

'There's a comic song I did on an album some years back – nothing to do with *The Dwight House*. Always works when I do it in cabaret. And the thing is – there's a funny chorus which you three could do.'

Charles was struck by how reasonable Kenny sounded. This wasn't just an ego trip; he was genuinely trying to come up with a way out of their current impasse.

'But what about the kitchen slapstick scene?' asked Danny.

'We drop the kitchen slapstick scene,' Kenny replied.

Danny looked as though he had been shot through the heart.

'So how're things going with the dialogue scenes?' said Bix Rogers.

Charles found it bizarre that such a question could be asked by the director about his own show. Bix was meant to be responsible for the whole production of *Cinderella*, but he was still focusing all his attention on the musical numbers. Presumably at some point during rehearsals, Charles comforted himself, they'd have to do a run of the whole show, and then Bix would see the uneven quality of the dialogue scenes. How the director reacted then would be interesting.

'We're getting there,' Kenny replied, 'but there's a lot of work still to be done.'

'I'm sure there is.' But Bix spoke as if, whatever the nature of the work that needed doing, it was somebody else's problem, rather than his.

'We've been working on the kitchen slapstick scene.'

'Oh yes,' Bix responded distractedly.

'Danny's very keen to keep it in, but I'm not sure it's going to play right.'

'Well, see how you go.'

'I was suggesting to the boys that maybe we junk the slapstick scene and put in another musical number.'

Bix's eyes lit up. 'Now that is a good idea.'

Felix was not to be upstaged. 'I was thinking also, Bix, that I could put in a bit of my stand-up act too . . . you know, in that bit when I'm alone in the kitchen just before Cinderella goes to the ball. I've got a very funny routine about being gay and shopping for vegetables.'

'Sure. Whatever works,' said the director.

A second bullet appeared to have entered Danny's heart. Charles, who also had great respect for the traditions of pantomime, felt for him. He thought back to the pantomimes he and Frances had taken their daughter Juliet to, back in the days when their marriage and family life had been almost normal. And that of course made him think again about Frances, and the terrible prospect of losing her.

Rehearsal breaks in the two halls of St Asaph's Church didn't always coincide, but they had done that morning, so the musical parts and the dialogue parts of the company were all foregathered in the larger hall. Except of course for a lot of the dancers, who had gone straight outside to light up cigarettes.

One who hadn't gone, though, was the dance captain, Jasmine del Rio. Though everyone had been introduced at the start of rehearsals, the dancers hadn't intermingled a lot with the acting members of the company. It was partly because they always tended to stick together, but also because the intensity of Bix Rogers' choreographic rehearsals left them little chance to socialize.

But at this coffee break Jasmine del Rio detached herself from Kitty Woo and came across purposefully to join the sycophantic group surrounding Kenny. Charles was struck again by the beautiful suppleness of her body and by the hardness of her face. He found it impossible to put an age on her. From a distance eighteen, closer at least thirty.

Jasmine carried a cup of coffee and deliberately took the vacant chair next to Kenny. 'We haven't been introduced properly, have we?' she said. Her voice had that kind of slack American twang affected by some on the outskirts of show business.

He smiled his Dwight Bredon smile, open and welcoming. 'No, we haven't. I've seen you across a crowded rehearsal room, but that's all.' He held out a hand. 'I'm Kenny Polizzi.'

It was a good ploy, which Charles had seen used by a lot of famous people in showbiz. Even though well aware that everyone in the entire world knew who they were, they demonstrated apparent humility by identifying themselves.

'Jasmine del Rio,' she said, taking his hand.

'It's an honour to meet you,' he said, still playing the humble card.

'Though actually we have met before . . . worked together.'

'Really?' Kenny looked puzzled and a little wary. Not recognizing someone he'd worked with might tarnish his image of 'regular guy' bonhomie. It might even make him look a bit starry. 'When was this?'

'More than fifteen years ago. Before the whole *Dwight House* thing began.'

'Oh.' He looked relieved. Maybe forgetting someone after fifteen years wasn't so bad.

'Besides,' she went on, 'I wasn't called Jasmine del Rio then.'

'Oh? What were you called?'

She smiled lazily, delaying the impact of her words. Then she said, 'Marybeth Docker.'

It was fortunate that Bix called everyone back to rehearsal at that point, because it obscured Kenny's reaction to the name. But Charles was near enough to see that the American looked as though he had been slapped in the face, very hard.

As had now become a habit, Charles lingered by the exit to St Asaph's Church Halls until Kenny joined him. Going to the pub together had quickly become an evening ritual for the two men. Charles still couldn't help wondering whether it was a self-imposed test for Kenny, a proof to himself of how completely he had defeated the temptation of the demon drink.

That evening as they left the hall, they encountered a woman standing outside in the street. Of indeterminate age, she wore a lilac hooded waterproof and sequin-decorated jeans. She had a small wheeled suitcase in a tiger-skin design. Her face was caked with powdery make-up and thick glasses distorted her eyes. For some reason he couldn't define, Charles felt there was something odd about her.

But clearly the woman knew Kenny Polizzi, and he knew her.

'Hello,' she said. 'I found you.' Her accent was American.

'You always do, Gloria.' He spoke cautiously, warily, as if he knew that saying the wrong thing could upset her.

'I sure do,' the woman agreed.

'This is Charles Paris. He's in the show too.'

'Hi,' she said abstractedly. She clearly had no interest in Charles.

'Will you be staying here in Eastbourne?' asked Kenny with something like foreboding.

'Oh yes, sure. I've booked in. I'll be here for the duration of the show.'

'Right.' Nervously, Kenny asked, 'Which hotel have you booked into?' Clearly he was worried she might have found out he was staying in the Grand and followed him there.

So he looked very relieved when she replied, 'I'm in a very nice clean bed and breakfast.' He looked a little less happy when she continued, 'Very near here, near where you're rehearsing, Kenny. So I'll be very close. Like I always am. You know I'm always here for you, Kenny. Or should I say "Dwight"?'

'Whichever.' There was an awkward silence. At least it felt awkward to Charles. But the woman seemed unaffected. She just stood, blinking at her idol.

Kenny broke the impasse. 'Well, Charles and I must be moving, Gloria.'

'Sure.' She stepped back. 'I'll see you tomorrow, Kenny.'

When they were out of earshot Charles looked quizzically at Kenny. 'Your Number One Fan?'

'Kind of.'

'Harmless, I hope.'

'So do I. And I'm pretty sure she is. Don't think she's about to chop my legs off. No, Gloria's just a bit of a fruitcake. She usually manages to find out where I am going to be, and she just . . . rolls up there.'

'Even when it's in another country?'

'Yeah. She's got some kind of trust fund. Money's not a problem for her.'

'But is she a problem for you?'

Kenny shrugged. 'People like Gloria van der Groot are occupational hazards for someone in my position.'

'She's a stalker?'

'You could call it that. But she's not really too much hassle. She doesn't ask anything of me – not like some of the weirdos I get mail from. She just . . . likes to be near me, I guess. She's never done anything that makes me feel I should call the cops. I've never had to get Lefty in to start handing round the injunctions. Gloria is just obsessed with *The Dwight House* – or with my character in *The Dwight House*. It's not me she's after, just some fictional guy on the television.'

They had reached the door of the pub. Suddenly Kenny drew back. 'I won't be joining you tonight. Got a few things need sorting out.'

'Fine,' said Charles, but he was already speaking to his friend's retreating back.

He didn't know whether it was seeing Gloria van der Groot . . . or his earlier encounter with Jasmine del Rio . . . or an anxiety that Charles knew nothing about . . . but something had rattled Kenny Polizzi.

FIVE

BARON HARDUP: My wife and I were perfectly happy for twenty-five years. Then we met each other.

'But it makes nonsense of the story,' said Danny Fitz. 'Not to mention the tradition.'

'Look, Kenny is the biggest name in this show,' said Bix Rogers. 'Nobody's going to argue with that, are they?'

'I'm not arguing with that,' said the Ugly Sister. 'He's a name that's known throughout the world, but that's not the point.'

'Then what is the point?'

'The point is that Baron Hardup – whoever's playing the part – is still a minor role in the story of *Cinderella*. And there is a traditional pecking order in the Walkdown.'

The Walkdown was what they were rehearsing that morning. This is the climax of every pantomime, when all the cast, in new costumes (or not in new costumes, according the exigencies of the production's budget), parade from the back of the stage to the front to receive – and milk – the audience's applause.

Because this moment in the show involved the entire cast, Bix was actually giving some direction to the speaking company members as well as the singers and dancers, a novelty so far in the rehearsal process. And, needless to say, he wanted the show's finale to be a really big production number. This was bad news for Charles. Though he could just about hold a tune and get away with singing onstage (particularly singing with other people – he'd got very good over the years at synchronizing his lips and letting no sound emerge), dancing was another matter.

He could move all right, learn the steps that he was meant to be doing . . . so long as there was no music playing. Once the accompanist or band started, he was put off his stroke completely. It had been ever thus. From Oxford University revue onwards, Charles Paris had been the despair of a lengthening line of musical directors and choreographers. And since at auditions for the

Empire Theatre Eastbourne's *Cinderella* he had blithely assured the director that he could sing and dance, he wasn't looking forward to the moment when Bix found out the truth.

Lying at auditions, incidentally – or to put it more graciously, finessing the truth – is so common among actors that very few of them feel any guilt about it. After all, what matters is getting the part and if a few inexactitudes are involved in that process . . . well, surely it's in a good cause. Age is one of the subjects where a little laxity with the truth is almost *de rigueur*. Charles had an actor friend from university – so an exact contemporary in his late fifties – who, on being asked his age at auditions always replied with touching sincerity, 'Forty-one, but play younger.'

And of course, when it comes to special skills, actors' claims are often way wide of the mark. There are many true stories of film actors who, having bigged up their equestrian abilities through a long sequence of casting interviews, encountered a horse for the first time on the day the movie started shooting. And Charles particularly relished the story of an American actor who, asked at an audition whether he was Jewish, replied, 'Not necessarily.'

So he didn't feel guilty about the lies he'd told Bix, but he anticipated a certain awkwardness when they got to his part in the choreography of the Walkdown.

Still, mercifully, at that moment Bix was preoccupied by his argument with Danny Fitz. The point of contention was the order in which the last few characters should appear in the Walkdown. 'This is nothing to do with billing, Bix,' Danny continued. 'It's just the way *Cinderella* has always been done. You start the Walkdown with the chorus boys and girls, then the minor characters – like the Broker's Men, Dandini, that lot – usually in twos. Then the last few entrances are Baron Hardup and the Fairy Godmother, quite often coming on together. Next comes Buttons, on his own. Then the two Ugly Sisters – and, finally, in their wedding finery, Prince Charming and Cinderella! That's the way it's always been.'

'Well, it's not going to be in this production,' Bix Rogers announced with uncharacteristic firmness. 'Kenny Polizzi will be the last person to make an entrance in the Walkdown.'

'But it doesn't make sense for—'

'It's going to happen, Danny. Kenny's contract guarantees him top billing – and top billing includes taking the final entrance for the Walkdown.'

Charles could recognize there was no way round that argument and, with bad grace, Danny was forced to accept it too.

The public nature of this discussion was possible because its subject, Kenny Polizzi, was not present at rehearsal that Friday morning. He was guesting on a daytime television chat show. The management of *Cinderella* recognized that, since his work-load in the pantomime was light, he was best employed drumming up publicity for the production.

Kenny's absence from St Asaph's Church Halls that morning prevented – or probably only delayed – an encounter that Charles would have given a great deal to witness.

It was getting towards lunchtime, and it had been a gruelling morning – particularly for Charles. He would have thought, given the time pressures on the rehearsal schedule, that Bix, having taken on board the patent fact that Charles had more left legs than a centipede, would have endeavoured to simplify the steps that he wanted this particular Broker's Man to make. But that was not the Bix Rogers way. For one thing he was a perfectionist. He had a very clear idea in his mind of every move he wanted every character to make during the musical numbers and he wasn't going to allow the basic incompetence of one of his cast to spoil the vision.

But Bix was also one of those worrying people (worrying to Charles, anyway) who constantly expressed the view that 'everyone can dance'. While this might be a good approach with primary school children and could even encourage some of the more inhibited to have a go, it was never going to work on Charles Paris. So, particularly for Charles and Bix, it was a tough morning.

They'd got to the point when the director said, 'A little bit more tinkering, then one more run at it and we'll break for lunch,' when the doors of the rehearsal room burst open.

It was really no surprise that Lilith Greenstone knew how to make an entrance. She was one of those rare child stars in the movies who'd survived to become an adult star in the movies.

She had also diversified into stage work, revealing that, unlike many film actors, she could actually act. Sing and dance, too. She'd recently won an Emmy for her work in a Broadway musical.

And when she burst into that rehearsal room in Eastbourne everything stopped. Everyone was silent. They just looked at her.

She was quite a sight to see. Workouts with a personal trainer, expert attention to her jet-black hair and punctiliously applied make-up ensured that she looked fifteen years younger than her real age of forty-eight. Her olive-coloured eyes sparkled with life. A green dress in some shiny material stopped way up her thighs, revealing perfect black-stockinged legs which ended in short mushroom-grey boots. Over the ensemble a white faux-fur coat reached almost to the ground. To Charles Paris, she looked pretty amazing.

And if there was anyone in the rehearsal room who hadn't recognized her, Lilith Greenstone's first words might have helped the identification process. 'Where,' she demanded, 'is that bastard husband of mine, Kenny Polizzi?'

It said something for the power of stardom that no one thought to reprimand her. Anyone else who had broken up a rehearsal like that – particularly someone who knew the usages of theatre – would have been immediately bawled out.

And Bix, who as director should have been the one bawling Lilith Greenstone out, was all over her like a rash. A real Broadway musical star – right there in his own rehearsal room. Though not actually gay, Bix demonstrated all the camp reverence accorded to such mythical creatures.

'I'm so sorry, Miss Greenstone,' he said, before even introducing himself, 'I'm afraid Kenny hasn't been called for rehearsal today. He's in London doing a chat show.'

'Jeez!' said Lilith. 'You mean I could have gone straight to London, rather than dragging down here to Hicksville-on-Sea?'

'Kenny should be back here this evening,' said Bix in a conciliatory tone.

'Then I'll hang around for the bastard,' said Lilith.

The director, excited that she might mean she was going to hang around the rehearsal, saw an opportunity to impress her with his choreographic skills. 'We were just about to break for lunch,' he said. 'Just after we've done one more run of the show's closer. Would you like to see us do that?'

'Hell, no,' she replied. 'What I want to see is a large drink. And I'm starving hungry too. I can't eat that crap they serve on airplanes. Is there one of your traditional English pubs in this back-end of nowhere?'

'Yes, of course there is, Miss Greenstone. And it would give me great pleasure to take you there once I've just finished rehearsing this number. Now if you—'

'I want a drink *now*,' said Lilith implacably.

'Ah. Well.' Bix's rehearsal plans were instantly rescheduled. He clapped his hands. 'OK, everyone, that's a wrap for this morning.' He hadn't used the word 'wrap' to them before. Charles reckoned he just wanted to appear movie-savvy to Lilith.

He wasn't the only one who asked Bix if he was going to come back to rehearse the Walkdown again after lunch. If they weren't, Baron Hardup wasn't called for the afternoon and he would be free. The director said no, after the break he'd be moving on to the Fairy Godmother transformation scene.

Bix escorted Lilith to the pub, glowing with the reflected glory of the stardust she scattered over him. Charles went to the pub too. But his journey had nothing to do with Lilith Greenstone. He would have gone there anyway.

After half an hour in the Sea Dog, Charles was beginning to get a little sick of Bix's sycophancy. And from the occasional look in Lilith's eyes he got the impression she was beginning to tire of it too. Fine to have her work appreciated, flattering that Bix could provide such detail of every show she had been in, but there was a limit to how much flattery she could take. Charles sensed they were both relieved when the director regretfully said he had to return to rehearsal.

By then they were two rounds of drinks in. Charles had knocked back a couple of large Bell's, and Lilith had kept pace with large vodka tonics. At Bix's departure both of them seemed to have found their glasses mysteriously empty. 'Same again?' asked Charles.

'Sure. And I'm still starving hungry. What's that traditional pub meal you have over here? Sausage and hash?'

'Sausage and mash is the more usual dish on offer.'

'Get me one of them.'

At the bar Charles ordered sausage and mash for the both of them and the same again on the drinks, which he took back to the table.

As he sat down he covertly looked again at Lilith with a degree of amazement. She was so perfectly groomed she looked like a doll that had just been taken out of its display box. But no, that was the wrong image. She was a lot feistier than a doll. But still so perfectly presented. Almost too perfect to be fanciable, thought Charles. It was hard to imagine rolling about in bed with something so soigné. But maybe with a little practice he could imagine it.

'Have you just arrived today?' he asked. It was a question that hadn't been raised throughout Bix's toadying.

'Sure. Limo brought me straight down from Heathrow.'

'To confront Kenny?'

It struck Charles after he'd said it that the enquiry might be thought impertinent, but Lilith showed no signs of objecting. 'Sure. And I'm not leaving till I've got this divorce finalized.'

'Kenny did mention something about a disagreement between your lawyers.'

'Forget the lawyers. It's a disagreement between Kenny and me. Oh yeah, the lawyers have to sort out the details – at enormous cost – but basically it's down to Kenny and me, face to face.'

'I thought lawyers were there so that the two combatants don't actually have to meet face to face. That's certainly the way it works in England.'

'That's in theory the way it works in the States. But the lawyers move too slowly for my taste. I know it'll be more effective if I – using your word – "confront" Kenny.' There was relish in her voice at the prospect. 'You ever been through a divorce, Charles?'

'Erm . . . well . . . no.'

'This is my third. You could say I'm getting good at it.'

It was an echo of the line Kenny had used about his marriages on *The Johnny Martin Show*. Charles wondered which of the couple had come up with it first.

'What you just wouldn't believe, Charles,' Lilith went on, 'is how mean Kenny is. Mean in every sense of the word. He's fighting each tiny claim my lawyers make on him. He wasn't mean when I married him. What is it that happens to men when you marry them? All men. Or maybe, Charles –' she brought the full beam of her amazing eyes on to him – 'are you the exception that proves the rule?'

'Hardly.'

'But you said you hadn't been divorced. Does that mean you've been married for a long time?'

'It could mean I've never been married.'

'And does it?'

'No, it means . . . well . . .' And the prospect of defining the state of his marriage brought back the cold visceral anxiety about Frances's health.

'Well, I figure I've done marriage now. I guess I'll need men occasionally for sex, but I think I'll leave it at that. I don't want any more who're still there the next morning.'

At that moment their sausage and mash arrived. Lilith Greenstone asked the girl who brought them for 'a helluva lotta mustard', and dug into the meal like she hadn't seen food for a month.

When they'd got to the lip-wiping stage (which inexplicably didn't seem to affect the perfect outline of Lilith's painted mouth), she said, 'So, Charles, this is some kind of musical of *Cinderella* you're doing here?'

'It's not exactly that. It's a pantomime.'

'What? You mean black tights and white faces?'

Charles thought he was about to have to go through the full explanation routine he'd done with Kenny, but fortunately Lilith didn't seem that interested in the detail. Instead she went off at a tangent, suddenly asking, 'Is Kenny keeping off the booze?'

'Yes, he's being very good.'

'Firmly on the wagon?'

'Squeaky clean.'

'Huh. I pity whoever's around when he falls off.'

'You think he will?'

'Inevitable, Charles. Sure as night follows day. An addict like Kenny never stops being an addict.'

'Well, he's trying very hard. He's even found out where they have AA meetings here in Eastbourne.'

'Has he?' said Lilith. 'Damn.'

'Why damn?'

'If he was still drinking, it'd help the character assassination my lawyers are planning for him. Drink and drugs always help when you're building up a domestic-violence case.'

'Was there domestic violence in your marriage?' asked Charles, a little surprised. It didn't fit with the estimation he had formed of Kenny.

'My lawyers will say there was,' Lilith replied complacently. 'They're going to throw the whole lot at him. A guy beating up on his wife while under the influence of booze or drugs – that always plays well in a courtroom.'

'But is it true?'

'Charles, Charles . . .' She looked at him pityingly. 'The allegations Kenny and I are making about each other left the truth behind months ago. Hell, the stuff Kenny's been making up about my "cruelty" you just wouldn't believe.'

'But your lawyers have made charges of cruelty against him as well?'

'Sure they have. They're particularly building up the number of times he threatened me with a gun.'

'And did he?'

'He liked guns. He had plenty of them. Who's to deny that in the privacy of the marital home he didn't threaten me with one?' She focused her shrewd eyes on to Charles's. 'Has Kenny got a gun over here?'

'I wouldn't know,' he lied.

'I'll bet he has. Kenny feels naked without a gun. He'll have got Lefty Rubenstein to organize one for him. You met Lefty?'

'Yes, I have.'

'He does everything for Kenny, right down to wiping his ass.'

'Is he representing Kenny in the divorce proceedings?'

'No, but lawyers from his company are doing it. Lefty's too busy tending to Kenny's day-to-day demands. Which is good, because Lefty's way ahead the brightest in his company, and Kenny's divorce case is being looked after by incompetent underlings. Which means I've got far better lawyers than Kenny has. So I'm going to win.'

'How do you define "win" in a divorce?'

'Purely in financial terms. The amount of money my lawyers manage to screw out of the bastard, that's what'll define my success.'

'But if you've got such good lawyers, I don't really see why you felt the need to fly over here to see Kenny.'

'I told you. I need to see him face to face. I've still got enough power over him to make him agree to my terms.'

'And if he doesn't agree?'

Lilith Greenstone let out a thick throaty chuckle. 'Then I'll kill the bastard!'

Their drinking session continued most of the afternoon. Once Lilith had indulged in a few cheery fantasies of how she'd shoot her husband with his own gun, they didn't talk further about the divorce. In fact, afterwards, Charles couldn't remember too well what they did talk about. There was a bit of discussion as to when Kenny was likely to be back from London, where he was staying, where Lilith might stay if, as seemed likely, she'd be in Eastbourne overnight. (As befitted his starring status, Kenny Polizzi was in the five-star Grand Hotel. Lilith, relishing confrontations, decided she would book in there too.)

They also talked about acting. And though they came from opposite ends of the showbiz spectrum – Lilith Greenstone a Hollywood and Broadway star, Charles Paris a jobbing actor whose name was never going to be above the title of anything – they found a lot in common as they discussed the idiocies and injustices of their chosen profession.

Charles found himself warming to Lilith. She could certainly hold her liquor; at no moment did she slur even the smallest word. And though nothing altered the fresh-out-of-the-box perfection of her appearance, further acquaintance revealed that underneath that lay a real, unaffectedly charming woman with a filthy sense of humour. While Charles had started the afternoon appreciating Lilith as a cunningly wrought work of art, by the end of it he was fancying her as a real woman. He even had the daring thought that she might be a little attracted to him too. And he was glad that they had exchanged mobile numbers.

What broke up their alcohol-fuelled *tête-à-tête* was the appearance in the pub of Lefty Rubenstein. 'Oh my God,' he said when he saw Lilith. 'It's true.'

'What's true, Lefty?' she drawled.

'That you're here.'

'I sure am.'

'I'll have to let Kenny know.'

'You do that. And fix up a meeting for him with me this evening.'

'I'm not sure that I—'

'Do it, Lefty. I assume you still have the role of Kenny's gofer? His Pooper-Scooper?'

The lawyer's sweaty face coloured with anger. 'I don't like that expression to—'

'Fix the meeting, Lefty. You should still have my cellphone number. Text me the time and place.'

'Kenny isn't going to like it,' said the lawyer, 'you being over here.'

'I have long since ceased to care what Kenny likes and doesn't like,' said Lilith Greenstone magisterially.

When the ringing of his mobile woke him it took Charles a moment or two to register where he was. And indeed what time of day it was. A quick look around told him that he was lying on the bed in his digs in Eastbourne. And a glance at his watch supplied 'nine-fifteen'. Since there was darkness outside the windows whose curtains he hadn't drawn, he assumed it was nine-fifteen in the evening.

'Hi, Charles,' said the voice at the other end of the line. 'It's Kenny.'

'Safely back from London?'

'Back, anyway. Charles, I need to see you. Meet me in the pub by the theatre – what's it called?'

'The Sea Dog.'

'Yeah. Soon as you can get there.'

It never occurred to Kenny Polizzi that anyone might not be free to answer one of his summonses. Charles, beginning to feel the headache brought on by his afternoon's excesses, meekly agreed to go straight to the pub.

'Good. See you there.'

The 'S' of the word 'see' sounded just the teensiest little bit slurred.

Was it possible that Kenny Polizzi was drunk?

SIX

BARON HARDUP: Don't drink and drive – this warning's real!
It slops all over the steering wheel.

It didn't take long for Charles's suspicion to be confirmed. On the table in front of Kenny was a row of empty tonic-water splits, a bucket of ice and a full glass. Charles could smell the vodka from the other side of the table. Kenny had very definitely fallen off the wagon. Charles remembered Lilith expressing pity for whoever was around when that happened. And he realized that he might have got the part. Kenny had marked him out as designated drinking partner.

'I'd offer to get you something from the bar,' said Charles, 'but it looks like you're sorted.'

'I am very definitely sorted.' Kenny took a long swallow from his glass. 'God, you forget how wonderful booze is . . . Just the taste of the stuff is a kind of heaven.'

Charles got himself a large Bell's and returned to the table. He was determined not to ask what had caused Kenny's backsliding. The last thing he wanted to do – or had any right to do – was to come across sounding censorious. If Kenny wanted to confide in him about the reasons for his broken resolution . . . well, that was a different matter entirely.

So Charles confined his opening conversational gambit to a raised glass and the word 'Cheers.'

The vodka glass was lifted and clinked against his. 'Your first drink of the day?' asked Kenny.

'Hardly.' Charles was grateful for the way his first sip of Bell's had started to melt away the headache he'd woken up with.

'Why,' said Kenny Polizzi in a way that was both bemused and wistful, 'why is it that women have such good memories?'

'I don't know,' Charles replied safely, letting his drinking companion direct the conversation in his own way.

'Every darned thing they seem to remember, every darned

thing. They got some kind of compartment in their brains men
don't have. Something rash you said to them, something thoughtless you did fifteen years ago, they remember every detail. They
store that stuff up and bring it out when you're at your most
vulnerable.'

Charles wondered what rash words or thoughtless deeds Lilith
had brought up at her meeting with Kenny. It must have affected
him pretty badly to get him back on the booze with such speed.

'Whereas men,' Kenny went on, 'we have a great capacity to
forget stuff. We don't brood about the past, we move on. If
something's broke, like a marriage or a relationship, we recognize
that it's gone and just move on . . .'

'To the next marriage or relationship?'

'Sure. Why not? You gotta keep hoping there's something
better round the next corner. Otherwise you might just as well
curl up your toes and die.'

This talk of marriages brought on another cold pang of anxiety
about Frances. But Kenny was in no mood to notice what Charles
might be feeling. He was off on his monologue. He only needed
an audience.

'I guess I kinda knew the stakes when I got into this business.
You get famous, that brings a lot of shit along with it. Certainly
you have to work damn hard to retain any privacy. Otherwise
every single member of the public reckons they're due a bit of
you. And now every single member of the public has got a camera
on their cellphone . . . and they can send their photos off on
Facebook or Twitter or . . . Jeez, there is no such thing as privacy
any more.

'Then if you've got money – or if you've had money – everyone
thinks they have rights to some of that too. They see in some
newspaper gossip column how much I was paid for each episode
of *The Dwight House*, and they think I must be rolling in the
stuff. They don't take into account the kind of expenses someone
in my position has, the number of people I have to employ just
to keep the Kenny Polizzi brand going. They don't think
about the pay-offs that come with three divorces. It never occurs
to them that some people are just bad with money. Like me. It
wouldn't matter how much money I had, I'd still lose it all in
misplaced generosity and rash purchases and dodgy investments.

That's what happened with me. Then I got involved in gambling, and you can sure as hell build up big debts very quickly there. And the people who want those debts paid aren't necessarily the nicest people in the known universe.'

Charles remembered something Kenny had said when they first met. 'Are you talking about the Mafia?'

The American chuckled. 'Well, I might be. But people who know about these things tell me you shouldn't talk about the Mafia. Safer not to.'

After that enigmatic reply he sighed. 'But that's just how I am. Bad with money. And yet people are always trying to squeeze more out of me. More of what I don't have.'

Having met Lilith, Charles could imagine just the kind of pressure she had put on her soon to be ex-husband. It really was no surprise that he'd fallen so dramatically off the wagon.

Kenny Polizzi's rant had spiralled down to melancholy silence. Then suddenly he looked at his drinking companion and demanded, 'Do you do drugs, Charles?'

'No. Tried pot . . . cannabis . . . whatever you want to call it . . . a couple of times in my twenties. Just gave me a splitting headache.'

'And never anything stronger?'

Charles Paris shook his head, feeling almost apologetic for his lack of experimentation. His hadn't been such a wild life, really. He hadn't got any vices . . . well, except for the Bell's. And maybe young actresses . . . though it had been a while since one of them had been around.

'No problemo,' said Kenny Polizzi. His mobile phone rang. He checked the display and said, 'Well, there's synchronicity for you.' He pressed the green button. 'Hi, Lefty. That's good. I knew I could rely on you. Where are you? OK, I got that. I'll find him.'

He picked up his coat, from whose pocket a vodka bottle poked out, and looked at his companion. 'Night's only just starting, Charlie boy. You going to join me for the rest of it?'

'You mean you're going to continue drinking somewhere else?'

'You could say that. Yes, that is my plan. One of my plans, anyway. You going to join me?'

Charles was tempted. He'd got to that point of drunkenness

where continuing to drink was a very attractive option. But he was also in the rare situation (for him) of being in work. He was called for *Cinderella* rehearsals the following morning. He had spent the whole afternoon drinking with Lilith Greenstone. And he was getting to the stage of his life when he didn't bounce back from hangovers with the Wobbly Man resilience he had once possessed.

'I think I'd better say no, Kenny.'

'Oh.' Baron Hardup looked a little put out. He wasn't used to people not going along with his suggestions. 'Party pooper,' he said, but he didn't bother to muster any other arguments. Instead, saying, 'See you soon,' Kenny tightened his hold on the neck of his vodka bottle and walked out of the pub.

SEVEN

FAIRY GODMOTHER: Come, Cinders, you must take my hand,
For there is evil in this land.

The television at Charles Paris's digs offered disappointingly thin fare that evening. As it did most evenings. In Charles's view the worst thing that ever happened to television was when it started letting ordinary people onto its programmes. Ordinary people were ordinary for a very good reason – because they weren't very interesting. To feature them in quiz games and make documentaries about them seemed to him the surest way of making dull programmes. It also meant there were fewer outlets for professionals . . . in other words actors like Charles. Not to mention writers and . . . so in his mind the whole cycle of grievance began again.

That evening he found himself watching some tedious fly-on-the-wall documentary about bakers – how early they had to get up in the morning, how proud they were of their work, how merrily they joshed with their fellow workers. Who cared anything about bakers? What they did did not come under the definition of 'interesting'.

But then nor did so many other subjects that television programmes were made about. Cooking . . . gardening . . . to Charles these were seriously dull activities. And now they even made programmes about the dullest and most frustrating of all human activities – house purchase.

With a few drinks inside him, he could wax quite eloquent at the shortcomings of television. Charles knew he was getting to the age where he was in danger of sounding crusty, but dammit, at his age he'd earned the right to be crusty.

Such thoughts recycled through his brain as he sat in his digs that evening, watching a baker demonstrating how he plaited dough, and sipping Bell's from the bottle.

Maybe he'd even dropped off to sleep again. Certainly he felt a bit disoriented when he heard his mobile ring.

'Hello?'

'Charles, it's Kenny.' The voice was slurred and also slightly panicky.

'What's up?'

'I need you to help me, Charles. I need you here.'

'Where's here?'

'I'm under the pier.'

'Under the pier?'

'Yes. Come here quickly!'

Charles mumbled that he would. He looked at his watch. God, he had been asleep. It was after one o'clock in the morning. At least, thank God, he hadn't undressed for bed.

He had a pee, took a long swallow of Bell's to brace him for whatever lay ahead, and went out into the darkness. It had got a lot colder since he had returned to his digs, so after a couple of hundred yards he went back to fetch his ancient duffel coat (the one that made him look like some plucky naval officer in a British movie almost definitely featuring John Mills – and probably Jack Hawkins as well).

Eastbourne was almost eerily empty at that time of night. Against the sighing background of sea the silence was broken by the sound of individual cars, but Charles didn't see any as he made his way towards the pier. He gathered his duffel coat around him, realizing with a slight shock that it was now the first of December.

There was still nobody about when he got to the entrance. A deep throbbing from the Atlantis Club's Friday Nighter at the far end of the pier showed that there were young people out there dancing to local DJs. But the more insistent sound was the sea washing restlessly and relentlessly, shifting the shingle some way below him. Charles did not see a living soul at street level.

Nor did he see a living soul when he went down the steps and looked underneath the pier.

No living soul, no. But Kenny Polizzi lay there, half-propped against one of the pier supports.

His wig was crooked. There wasn't much blood, but there was a neat bullet hole in the centre of his forehead.

EIGHT

FIRST BROKER'S MAN: Have you heard the news? Would you like a bulletin?
SECOND BROKER'S MAN: No, I think I'd rather have a bullet out.

Charles felt three things. First, he felt immediately sober. Second, he felt a degree of guilt. If he'd arrived at the pier quicker, if he hadn't gone back to get his duffel coat, he might have been in time to save Kenny from his fate.

But his third feeling was the strongest – an overpowering urge to run away from the scene of the crime. He didn't want the complications of suspicion and police enquiries. He wanted to be back in his digs, curled up under his duvet, fast asleep.

But a little rational thought told him that he couldn't escape so easily. There was no getting away from the fact that he was the person who had found Kenny's body. And there was almost definitely evidence somewhere that would prove that fact. He'd probably been recorded on CCTV cameras during the walk from his digs to the pier. And his mobile number would be one of the last that had been called from Kenny's phone. There was no way round it. He would have to face the music.

Reluctantly, but resigned to his situation, Charles Paris rang 999.

As he had anticipated, it was a long night. A panda car arrived at the pier entrance level less than ten minutes after his call. But that was just the start of a procession of more police vehicles. Soon the pier was illuminated by blue flashing lights. The two uniformed cops who had first arrived were quickly joined by a lot of plain-clothes officers, all with different tasks to complete. And the task for two of them, one male and one female, was to question Charles Paris. Once they had looked over the scene of crime with him, they took him into a police van for questioning.

Meanwhile the wild night of the youngsters in the Atlantis Club was curtailed prematurely by the arrival of the police. Names were taken and they were all sent on their way home. Most of the young people assumed it was a raid searching for drugs and dealers. None of them realized the significance of the police tape shutting off the steps down to sea level.

Though extremely courteous, there was no doubt that there was a level of suspicion in the manner of the cops who inter-rogated Charles. This came as no surprise to him. He, after all, was probably the first person to discover Kenny's body, and the shallowest familiarity with crime fiction would tell anyone that the person who finds the body is always high on the list of suspects.

So, very patiently, he went through the minutiae of his even-ing's encounters with Kenny. Though he no longer felt drunk – shock had shaken that out of him – the blinding headache had returned and Charles just felt incredibly tired. He still longed for the embrace of the duvet back at his digs.

But there was a lot more questioning to go. And of course they wanted him to provide contacts for the Empire Theatre management, for Bix Rogers and anyone else connected to Kenny. Charles mentioned Lefty Rubenstein, apologizing that he didn't have a phone number for him. He also said that he thought Lilith was staying at the Grand Hotel. The detectives made notes and passed no comments on his answers. He hadn't really taken in the names of his interrogators, but at some point they were joined by a small Asian woman called Detective Inspector Malik. She wore a trim charcoal-grey trouser suit and was evidently senior to the others. Hers was the card he was given with contact numbers, and she it was who urged him to get in touch if he remembered any further details, however apparently trivial.

A pale uncertain dawn was coming up over the grey Eastbourne sea when Charles was finally allowed to leave the van. He was also told by Detective Inspector Malik to inform the police if he was likely to leave Eastbourne – and he was pretty clearly discour-aged from doing so. All of his contact with the police had been polite and temperate, but he was left in no doubt that suspicions would automatically attach themselves to anyone connected with the crime scene.

Checking his watch, Charles realized that his interrogation had lasted nearly four hours. And during his incarceration in the police van television crews had arrived. They were kept on the upper level of the pier entrance by swathes of yellow and black tape, but the fact that they had appeared at all suggested that the news of the crime had got out and the media vultures were gathering.

Charles reckoned they must have somehow discovered the identity of the victim.

The news that Kenny Polizzi had been shot was going to be a huge international story.

Charles was so exhausted that he just passed out as soon as he lay on his bed. No time to take his clothes off. He didn't even have the energy to get under the warmth of the duvet that he'd been promising himself.

He was meant to be called at ten for a *Cinderella* rehearsal, but after the events of the night, he didn't even know whether the show would still be going on. And he was too tired to set an alarm.

As a result, he woke at half-past twelve with an aching brain too big for his cranium and a mouth as dry as the Gobi desert. He felt totally wiped out and insanely hungry. But before he went out to satisfy his hunger and rehydrate himself, he switched on the television for the BBC *News*.

And yes, the death of Kenny Polizzi was a very big story indeed. Clips were shown from *The Dwight House*, there were photos of his wives including Lilith Greenstone, and there was even an extract from his recent appearance on *The Johnny Martin Show*.

No mention was made of how he had met his end, just the news that his body had been found on the seafront at Eastbourne. The police were clearly trying to control the amount of information they released. Once it was publicly known that he had been shot, a whole new media frenzy would be unleashed.

Charles Paris wasn't very good at checking his mobile for messages, and it wasn't until he had reached the Sea Dog and ordered an irrigating pint that he looked at the phone. He knew he probably should have gone first to the St Asaph's Church

Halls to check whether rehearsals for *Cinderella* were continuing that day, but a beer and something to eat were greater priorities. He ordered fish and chips to go with his pint.

To his relief he found there was no message from the police. He felt sure they would be wanting to question him further, but at least that hadn't happened yet.

There was a message, however, from Bix Rogers, asking him to call as soon as possible. So after he'd finished his first pint – which didn't seem to touch the sides – and armed himself with a second one, he rang the director.

'Charles, presumably you've heard the news about Kenny?'

'Hard to avoid it.' No need yet to reveal that he was the one who had found the body.

'Well, look, obviously this puts us in a spot about the show.'

'I can believe that.'

'I've cancelled rehearsals for today.'

'Yes,' said Charles in a way that implied he already knew that.

'But the fact remains that we open in less than a week and we currently don't have a Baron Hardup.'

'No.'

'Now Kenny was a very big name, but I'm not trying to replace him with another big name. He's already got lots of publicity for our *Cinderella*, and the fact that he's dead is going to get us a whole lot more. So he's served his purpose and there's no need to replace like with like. It doesn't matter who plays Baron Hardup now. So I'd like you to take the part, Charles.'

It wasn't the most gracious job offer Charles had ever received, but it was still a perverse kind of good news. 'Thanks very much, Bix. I'll do my best. In fact, I have played the part before.'

'Oh?' The director didn't sound very interested in this piece of information. 'Anyway, if you could have a look at the lines before rehearsal on Monday . . .?'

'Sure. Presumably I won't be doing Kenny's routine about *The Dwight House* and the song based on its signature tune?'

'No, of course you won't.'

'What, you'll replace it with something?'

'No, we'll cut it.'

'Won't that make the show short?'

'We'll fill in with another song from Tilly Marcus's album,' replied Bix, once again confirming just how far down the theatrical food chain Charles Paris was.

In spite of the reason why he'd got the job and the demeaning way that he had been offered it, Charles was quite chuffed about his elevation to the role of Baron Hardup. Even with substantial routines cut, it was still a better part than a Broker's Man. And the big bonus was that he'd be spared the Sisyphean task of trying to get some comic rhythm going with Mick 'The Cobra' Mesquito. So it was good news.

The arrival of the fish and chips rather dampened his mood. The chips had been cooked in an oven, but it was a long time since they had had any contact with their parent potatoes. And the fish itself was dry like a cardboard inner tube from a toilet roll encased in sandpaper. It seemed ironic that a pub within sight of the English Channel was serving fish which had probably spent as much of its life in a freezer as it had in the sea. And the peas were like the peas he remembered from school, hard as bullets.

'Hello, Charles. How're you doing?' He looked up to see Felix Fisher with a glass of red wine. 'Mind if I join you?'

'Be my guest.'

The comedian sat down opposite and raised his glass. He wore an outlandish red diamanté jacket and his full street make-up. 'Congratulations, Charles.'

'On what?'

'I gather you were the one who discovered Kenny's body.'

'News travels fast.'

'Sure does. And of course in crime fiction the person who discovers the body—'

'Is the first suspect for the murder. Yes, I know all that. But are we actually talking about a murder?'

'I'd say there wasn't much doubt about that. People don't often get bullet holes in their foreheads by accident.'

News had certainly been travelling fast. 'Where have you got your information from, Felix?'

'There's been a lot on Twitter about it.'

'Ah,' said Charles, in a manner which he hoped suggested he was conversant with the ways of Twitter. Which of course he wasn't. 'Did it say there that I found the body?'

'Yes.'

'Any other references to me?'

'Oh, a few people are being very rude.' Felix's mouth formed into a camp moue of disapproval. 'Some were suggesting that you topped him.'

'What? Why would I have done that?'

'Because you wanted to play Baron Hardup.'

'Yes, but—'

'And now you are playing Baron Hardup.'

Felix seemed to know everything. 'I agree,' said Charles. 'But if you really think that I would go to the lengths of murder to—'

'No, I don't think that.'

'Oh, good.'

'It's just that some people do.'

'People on Twitter?'

'Yes.'

'Can they be stopped from disseminating wild theories like that?'

'Oh no, you can't stop people saying whatever they want to on Twitter. I suppose you could tweet yourself and enter the discussion, put your side of the story.'

Even if he knew how to, Charles couldn't see himself following that instruction. 'And are there other theories on Twitter about who killed Kenny?'

'Oh yes, hundreds.' Felix let out a melodramatic sigh at the follies of humankind.

'Any you think make sense?'

'Well, the most popular one . . .'

'Yes?'

'. . . is that Kenny had these very big gambling debts and that's why he was killed.'

'Oh?'

'It was a Mafia hit.'

Charles couldn't stop himself from saying, 'In Eastbourne?'

NINE

NAUSEA: Your teeth are like stars.
DYSPEPSIA: You mean that they're bright?
*   You mean that they sparkle?*
NAUSEA: No, they come out at night.

The two pints and the cardboard fish and chips had helped to make him a bit more human, but he still felt totally knackered. So, when Felix wandered off 'to check out Eastbourne's antique shops – always looking ahead to when I run my own dinky little emporium in the Cotswolds', Charles made his way back to his digs for what he called 'doing the crossword' (though in fact it meant more catching up on sleep).

In the serenity brought on by another infusion of alcohol, he congratulated himself on not feeling too bad. The shock from the events he had witnessed the previous night had dulled a little, and he brought his mind to bear on the theory that Felix had put forward, namely that Kenny had been killed by the Mafia.

Well, the guy's surname was Italian, which might be of some relevance. And he had talked of having gambling debts and the fact that 'the people who want those debts paid aren't necessarily the nicest people around'. Then, when Charles had asked if he was referring to the Mafia, the response had been enigmatic, to say the least.

So maybe Felix's was a theory worth going along with for the time being . . . particularly because Charles was still too fuddled to have any other theories. Something still didn't ring true about it, though. If the Mafia really wanted to kill Kenny, surely they could have done it more easily in the States? Why go to the trouble of sending a hit man all the way over to England?

Unless, of course, they'd already got someone on the ground over here . . .? But somehow the idea of the Mafia having an active cell in Eastbourne seemed too incongruous to be anything but funny.

To clear his mind of such speculation Charles focused on the *Times* crossword. He managed to fill in one clue before passing out once again. And once again it was his mobile ringing that woke him up. He pressed the green button and mumbled a 'Hello'.

'It's Frances.'

'Oh, damn. It's Friday, isn't it? I promised I'd ring you.'

'Don't worry about that,' said Frances wearily. 'It's Saturday actually, and I never really thought you would.'

'Oh, but I . . .' No point in wasting time with excuses. 'You've had the result of the biopsy?'

'Yes.'

'And?'

There seemed to be a long silence before Charles heard the words: 'It's benign.'

'Oh God, that's wonderful, Frances. Brilliant news! How do you feel?'

'I don't really know at the moment. Feel a bit battered. I don't think I've realized how stressed I'd been about the whole business. To be quite honest, I feel rather flat.'

'No surprise, after the build-up of tension. Once that's released, you . . . well, it's like the kind of flatness you feel after a first night.'

'I'm sure it is, Charles,' said Frances with just a hint of irony in her voice.

'You've told Juliet and Miles?'

'Of course I have, Charles.'

'Well, I'm just ecstatic at the news. I've . . .' He paused. Over the years he had become wary of saying emotional things to Frances. Too often she'd come back at him with a perfectly justified put-down. But that day he thought it was worth the risk. 'Since we last spoke . . . since I heard about the biopsy . . . well, it's just made me realize how much you still mean to me.' He took a bigger risk. 'It made me realize how much I love you, Frances.'

'Well, that's nice,' she said. No words of reciprocation. But her tone was benign. Just like the result of the biopsy. It opened up the possibility to Charles that they might get back together on a more permanent basis. At some point. Which was comforting.

*   *   *

The news from Frances gave Charles a real lift. And, emerging from the shocks of the night before, he felt positively euphoric. He noticed it was already dark outside, and switched on the television to watch the six o'clock news.

The police had clearly released more information to the slavering press. In the days of social media extended secrecy on any subject had ceased to be an option. As soon as one person knew something, it was straight away potentially ready to be shared with the entire world. And by now the news had somehow slipped out that Kenny Polizzi had been murdered by a bullet in the forehead.

This made his death an even bigger story, definitely the lead item on the bulletin. More clips from *The Dwight House* were shown. More friends and associates were interviewed – even Bix Rogers got his moment in the media sun, which he clearly enjoyed hugely. Notable by their absence from the screen were Lefty Rubenstein and Lilith Greenstone. Charles wondered how they had reacted to the news.

He wasn't kept waiting long for an answer. Just as the newsreader had moved on to report possible financial meltdown in the Eurozone, he got a call on his mobile from Lilith.

'Charles, you've heard the news about Kenny?' she asked.

'I'd have to have buried myself in a bunker under seventeen layers of concrete not to have heard,' he replied.

'Right.'

'I'm sorry. I feel I should be offering you condolences or—'

'The hell with that. I hated the bastard. I'm not about to make with the crocodile tears.'

'But you must be feeling shock at the very least.'

A verbal shrug came from the other end of the line. 'Not so much shock. I'm just more aware of my good fortune.'

'Oh?'

'Look, Charles, the divorce hasn't come through. I am still the rightful Mrs Kenny Polizzi. Unless the bastard changed his will before the divorce was finalized – which I don't think he did – I'm no longer looking at a slice of his estate, I'm looking at the whole lot. Which I must say, having put up with Kenny for as long as I did, is no less than I deserve.'

'Have you spoken to the police?'

'Yeah. They talked to me.'

'Did they let slip any theories as to who might have shot him?'

'No, the cops here – and in the States too, though to a lesser extent – tend to play that kind of information close to their chests. I think they were just kinda checking I didn't pull the trigger.'

'And you managed to convince them you didn't.'

'I guess.'

Charles chuckled. 'And if I were to tell them I heard you saying you'd kill the bastard . . .?'

'I don't think it'd make too much difference to the way the cops are thinking. Besides –' her voice sank to a level of great sultriness – 'you're too much of an English gentleman to ever rat on me, aren't you, Charles?'

'I like to think so.'

'I like to think that maybe you'd like to join me for a drink at the Grand Hotel.'

'That sounds a very attractive idea, Lilith. When?'

'How's about right now?'

There was a uniformed policeman, lingering as unobtrusively as a policeman in uniform can, in the foyer of the Grand Hotel. No great surprise, when Charles thought about it. This was where the late Kenny Polizzi had been staying. This was where his still-current wife was staying. The hotel management might well need back-up to hold at bay inquisitive journalists or devastated fans. The thought made Charles wonder how Gloria van der Groot, Kenny's 'Number One Fan', had reacted to the news of her idol's death.

Except for the policeman's presence, a visitor to the hotel would have no inkling that anything untoward had happened to one of its guests. The Grand Hotel continued to be run with the quiet decorum that would be expected of a traditional five-star hotel on the south coast.

The girl he approached at the counter wore an immaculate grey suit and spoke good English, but with a marked Russian accent. Every hotel Charles had been into recently – which actually wasn't a great many – had seemed to be staffed entirely by people from the former Eastern Bloc.

It was with some trepidation that he said he was meeting Lilith

Greenstone. He was worried about being suspected of being one of the journalists or fans the policeman was there to deter.

But as soon as he said his name, there was no problem. The receptionist immediately said that Ms Greenstone was expecting him in the Debussy Suite, gave him the room number and directions to find the lift.

Of course it was quite logical that they should meet in her suite. Lilith Greenstone was, after all, very high profile. She might not be left in peace by the gawping public in one of the Grand Hotel's public rooms. But Charles Paris couldn't suppress a little flicker of excitement at the *tête-à-tête* that lay ahead.

He could never really believe that real people did live like they did in the movies. Deeply aware of his own inadequacies and vulnerabilities, he always assumed that everyone else was, like him, an assemblage of Achilles heels. But when Lilith let him into the seafront Debussy Suite, he really did feel like he was stepping into a movie.

The sitting room was splendidly lush, subtly illuminated by low table lamps. The windows were uncurtained, showing beyond the private balcony the lights of occasional ships plying the English Channel. The interior door was open, showing the passage to a bedroom. Charles glimpsed a huge bed with a kind of canopy over its head.

Lilith Greenstone too looked as if she had just stepped off a film set. Hair and make-up were perfect, as ever. So were the high heels and the midnight-blue wrap-around dress, which showed a generous amount of her already generous cleavage.

On the sitting-room table was a silver tray on which a bottle of champagne lolled in an ice bucket. It had already been opened. Lilith's flute was half-empty and she poured a full one for Charles.

'So,' she said as they sat down on the sofa facing the sea, 'let's raise our glasses to "No more Kenny".'

'Yes, all right, but I should say I did quite like the guy.'

'You weren't married to him.'

'That is undeniably true.'

They raised their glasses and clinked.

'And, like I said on the phone . . . condolences or whatever's appropriate to—'

'And like I said on the phone, no need.'

'Right. Fine.'

'So the cops have talked to you, Charles?'

'You bet. I was actually the one who found the body.'

'I heard that.'

'Whether I was the first person to find the body, though, who knows?'

'Howdja mean?'

'Well, not having actually witnessed the death, I don't know how many other people might have seen him.'

'Right, got you.'

'Mind you, the time frame was fairly short, between Kenny summoning me on the phone and my finding him.'

'How short?'

'Twenty minutes, half an hour tops.'

'OK. You have any thoughts who might have shot the bastard?'

Charles realized again that, beneath all the surface charm and sexiness, Lilith was a woman with an agenda. She had invited him to the Debussy Suite because there was information she wanted from him. Or maybe she wanted to know the extent of his ignorance.

'I haven't a clue,' he replied. 'You know a lot more about his background than I do. You know who might have had a grievance against him.'

'Yes, like me, for instance. If I started listing the grievances I had against Kenny, we could be here all night.' She smiles a deliberately provocative smile. 'That is assuming we're not here all night anyway.'

Charles didn't know how to respond. Maybe he was meant to come back with some slick movie-dialogue riposte, but it didn't feel right to him. Instead he said, rather formally, 'I'm working from the assumption that you didn't kill him, Lilith.'

She nodded in mock-approval. 'Good assumption.'

'But, as I say, you know a lot more about Kenny than I do. You're more likely to be able to come up with a list of suspects than I am.'

'Maybe. But I wanted to ask you if he'd been antagonizing anyone in your *Cinderella* company. Any bust-ups there?'

Charles shook his head slowly. 'No, Kenny seemed to get on

with everyone.' He decided not to mention the brief confrontation the star had had with Jasmine del Rio. No need to cast suspicion on an incident that was probably perfectly harmless. Until he had worked out what Lilith wanted from him, he decided to play things cagey.

'Yup, good old Kenny,' said Lilith. 'Everybody's buddy. The big star who doesn't act like a big star, the regular guy who nobody gets pissed with. And if he does inadvertently upset someone, then he always sends in Lefty Rubenstein to clear up the mess, smooth things over, pay a little hush money if necessary. Good old Kenny.'

'Well, I can't think of anyone in the *Cinderella* company who might have wanted to kill him.'

'You mean rehearsals have been completely harmonious?'

'That might be overstating it – I'm sure you know enough about working in the theatre to understand that – but the arguments that have come up . . . Kenny wasn't involved in any of them.'

'And, knowing how keen showbiz people are on gossip . . . are there theories around the company about who might have topped him?'

'Well, the only *Cinderella* cast member I've seen since the murder is of the view that it was a Mafia hit.'

Lilith Greenstone looked genuinely amazed. 'What the hell would the Mafia have to do with Kenny? Not everyone who's got an Italian surname is a "made man". They don't all qualify for *The Sopranos*.'

'Kenny suggested to me that he had substantial gambling debts . . .'

'That's certainly true.'

'And the people trying to reclaim them were not necessarily the most salubrious types.'

'Go along with that too. But we're still not talking Mafia. Kenny had these fantasies, saw himself as the big star. Bit of a Sinatra complex. He loved promoting the suggestion that he was tied up with the Mafia. Gave him some kind of macho kick.'

'But not true?'

'Totally untrue. The kind of thing he'd sound off about when he'd had a few drinks – or the odd line of cocaine – to anyone who'd listen. And Kenny could usually find somebody who'd listen . . . because of course he was Kenny Polizzi, star of *The Dwight House*. But nothing to do with the Mafia.'

'Do you mind if I ask you something personal, Lilith?'

The magnificent shoulders shrugged. 'What's personal?'

'Why did you marry Kenny?'

'Ah.'

'I mean, given that since I've met you you've said nothing about him that wasn't pure vitriol.'

'Charles, you say you haven't been divorced, but surely you know enough about life to realize that what you feel when you're coming out of a marriage is kind of different from what you feel when you go into it.'

'Yes, I can see that, but on our brief acquaintance you don't strike me as a woman who has a lot of illusions about life . . .'

'We all still have a few illusions, Charles – even the most hardbitten of us. And the image of marriage for a girl like me, brought up as a God-fearing Southerner, kinda looms over one's life. I'd done it twice and screwed up. I hoped the third time I could make it work. And Kenny was that much older, I thought he'd bring me a sense of security. I'm one of those lost girls whose daddy died young.' She was silent for a moment. 'He died of a heart attack just around the time I was making the awkward transition from child star to adult star. I guess I've been looking for a father figure ever since.'

'But Kenny doesn't seem natural casting as a father figure. You and him . . . it still seems unlikely somehow.'

'Not so unlikely. Even now I can acknowledge the guy had a lot of charisma. And after his hellraising days, he was seriously determined to turn over a new leaf. When we met, he was off the booze, off the drugs, he was genuinely wanting to start over. And I guess I was a part of the redemption process.'

'And would I be wrong,' Charles asked cautiously, 'to think that you saw Kenny as something of a project? You could civilize him, you could turn his personality around in a way that his previous wives had failed to?'

'You're quite shrewd, Charles,' said Lilith, and she patted him on the knee, rather in the way a dog might be congratulated for bringing the stick back. 'Yup, there was an element of challenge there. I guess I thought I could tame Kenny.' She sighed, then said, 'There's another thing too, Charles . . .'

'Oh?'

'Kenny was high-profile. Like me. The fact that big names in showbiz keep getting into relationships with each other is not just to keep the celebrity magazines salivating. It's also because you gravitate towards people who understand the system, who know about the pressures of trying to find some privacy in their lives. They know about the bodyguards, the security consultants, the discreet limo companies . . . all that garbage which may look to the outsider like extravagant pampering, but is actually necessary just to get through life as a celebrity. You hook up with someone who knows about all that shit, there's a lot less time wasted in explanations.'

'I can see that,' said Charles Paris, whose career had never required the services of bodyguards, security consultants or discreet limo companies, and was never likely to. 'So how long did the honeymoon with Kenny last?'

'Until he fell off the wagon. Which he managed to do within three weeks of the wedding.'

'He'd climbed back on it, though, hadn't he? Mr Squeaky Clean again. Or at least he had until yesterday.' All that got from Lilith was a snort of contempt. 'Can I ask – were you the cause of him falling off the wagon yesterday evening, Lilith?'

His words angered her. 'What the hell do you mean by that?'

'Well, from what you said in the pub, you were planning to have a confrontation with Kenny. Next time I hear from him, he's smashed out of his skull. It seems reasonable to think there might be a connection between the two events.'

'I didn't give him drink. I wouldn't do that. If Kenny having a drink was a reaction to our conversation, then that's not my fault.'

'So you did have your confrontation?'

'You bet we did. Here in this very room. I left a message on his cellphone to call me as soon as he got back to Eastbourne. Left a message for Lefty too. Even when we were married, I often had to go through Lefty to contact Kenny.'

'Have you heard from him since the news of Kenny's death?'

Lilith shook her head. 'He's going to be very upset. Lefty's always bitching about Kenny, but the guy's really his *raison d'être*. Take Kenny away and Lefty's like an empty glove puppet.'

'Do you mind if I ask what you and your husband talked about when he came here?'

'I don't mind. No secret about it. I told you I was going to talk to him about the divorce. That's exactly what I did.'

'And was it a . . . er, civilized discussion?'

Lilith smiled grimly. 'On my part, yes of course. Kenny, needless to say, was less gracious.'

'And would you say you reached a conclusion?'

'I reached a conclusion. I told Kenny my terms.'

'Did he agree to them?'

'No, but he'll come round. Or rather,' she corrected herself, 'he would have come round if he were still alive. As it is . . .' a vindictive smile played around her perfect lips '. . . things have been simplified considerably.'

'And when Kenny left you, did he seem upset enough to go back on the booze?'

'He was pissed with me. Who knows whether that's what caused him to break his pledge. In a way I'd be slightly surprised if it was.'

'Oh?'

'That was one of the issues between us. I always said he was too weak to stick to any resolution, that he was just basically a soak and, whatever fine intentions he might express, he'd revert to being a soak. So if he went back on the booze, that'd be kind of a vindication of what I've always been saying.'

'Hm.' Charles tapped his chin thoughtfully. 'Then I wonder if it was something that happened after he'd talked to you that caused him to backslide . . .?'

A shrug. 'Coulda been.'

'Kenny didn't say he was going to meet anyone else after he'd left you, did he?'

'No.'

'No.' There was a silence. 'And, Lilith, do you have any theory yourself as to why Kenny might have been killed?'

Another shrug. 'Being in the wrong place at the wrong time? A mugging turned nasty? Getting mixed up with drug dealers?'

'Why do you say that? Do you know that Kenny had dealings with drug dealers here in Eastbourne?'

'No, but I know what happened other times when he fell off the wagon. He hits the vodka first, then suddenly he's got a desperate desire for coke. Once Kenny starts boozing, he's pretty soon on to his drug dealer . . . or he's on to Lefty to get on to his drug dealer. Here I guess he doesn't have a drug dealer, so here maybe he has to take risks if he's going to have to get his coke. So he finds himself in the company of one of Eastbourne's undesirables and . . .' Another shrug seemed to encompass everything else that might have happened.

Charles's first thought was that a genteel middle-class town like Eastbourne doesn't have 'undesirables', but then he realized he was out of date. These days everywhere has drug dealers.

They both seemed to relax. Each had got as much information from the other as they thought was probably available. Lilith refilled their glasses, firmly placed the bottle back in its ice bucket and focused those olive-coloured eyes on Charles's. At the same time her hand landed smoothly on his knee.

'Now,' she said, 'are we going to bed?'

Even in the throes of physical passion Lilith Greenstone didn't lose the perfection of her appearance and style. The sex was very good, and she certainly knew exactly what she wanted. So much so that Charles even had the sense of being a little marginalized. It wasn't that he felt that strongly about being in charge in bed, but he did like to feel he had some input into the decision-making process.

TEN

*FIRST BROKER'S MAN: What do call a policeman who's
   blonde on top?*
*SECOND BROKER'S MAN: Of course I know that – it's a
   fair cop!*

As Saturday night melted into Sunday morning and Charles
Paris walked along the front towards his digs he felt a
mixture of reactions. They included a not entirely admirable masculine cockiness. He felt he'd been put through a test
by Lilith Greenstone and he had not been found wanting. And
it had been a while since he'd actually had any sex, so it was
good to know that everything was in working order. There was
an unworthy glee too, derived from the fact that he'd just been
to bed with someone famous. Though he knew it was pathetic
to think like that – he of all people shouldn't be impressed by
celebrity – he couldn't help himself.

But there was also a less pleasant sensation, a feeling that the
whole exercise had had a clinical quality to it. Lilith was an
expert lover and, while not ungenerous, knew exactly how to
provide her own satisfaction. Which had left Charles at moments
feeling like little more than an animated dildo.

And then there had been a formal quality to the way she had
dismissed him. He knew from their earlier conversation that she
no longer wanted men who were 'still there the next morning',
so he hadn't been surprised when she called a halt to proceedings, announcing that she'd still got a bit of jet lag and needed
to catch up with her sleep. But Lilith's tone had been almost
peremptory. There was certainly not even a pretence that anything
emotional had been involved in their coupling.

All in all, Charles decided it was an experience he would
rather have had than not had. He'd needed sex and it had been
good sex. He'd acquitted himself well. It would be interesting
to see whether there would be any repeat of the encounter. He

knew that if there was to be there'd be no decision required from him on the matter. Lilith would make that call. And if she did make it, he thought he would be up for a return fixture.

It wasn't till he was getting into the bed at his digs that Charles thought about Frances. And remembered the huge relief that her call had brought to him. The biopsy had proved that the growth was benign. She didn't have breast cancer. It was partly the euphoria brought on by that news which had made him feel so good about going to bed with Lilith.

And the thought that, in relation to Frances, he should have felt guilty about that encounter didn't enter Charles Paris's head.

A call on his mobile woke him at nine the next morning. Exhaustion and the large amount of Bell's consumed before finally passing out left him a little muzzy and he didn't recognize the polite, purposeful female voice until she identified herself as Detective Inspector Malik.

She wanted to talk to him further, either at his digs or in the suite of rooms in the local station they had requisitioned as an incident room. Charles chose the police option. Even though he was living in an anonymous self-catering apartment, he was resistant to the idea of the cops coming knocking at his door.

Detective Inspector Malik was as courteous as she had been at their previous meeting and saw him supplied immediately with a cup of coffee. She introduced a male uniformed officer in the corner of the room, whose name Charles instantly forgot, and asked if he had any objections to their conversation being recorded.

He said he hadn't, eager to be as cooperative as possible. Even though he knew himself to be completely innocent, the prospect of being questioned by the police brought the same instinctive sense of guilt as an imminent visit to the headmaster's study back in his schooldays.

Detective Inspector Malik explained that their investigations were proceeding in a number of different directions. The fact that the murder victim was a foreign national complicated matters, and her team would shortly be joined by detectives who were flying over from the States. (Charles was interested that she referred to a 'murder'. But since the word had been on the television news and was now splashed all over that morning's Sunday papers that presumably was now the official line on the investigation.) The inspector emphasized how much she appreciated Charles's cooperation and insisted that there was nothing sinister about this second bout of questioning. All she and her team were trying to do was to get as detailed a picture as they could of the sequence of events on the night of Kenny Polizzi's death.

'Could we go back,' asked Detective Inspector Malik after all of this preamble had been completed, 'to the call you had from Mr Polizzi on the Friday night?'

'Of course,' replied Charles, still eager to be the class goody-goody.

Detective Inspector Malik consulted some notes on her iPad. 'According to what you told us last time we spoke, Mr Polizzi said that he needed you to help him.'

'Yes. That's exactly what he said.'

'Did you have any idea in what way he needed help?'

'No.'

'So why did you immediately do as he requested?'

'Well, wouldn't that be a normal reaction from anyone?' asked Charles, a bit tentative.

'It might be a normal reaction in different circumstances. But the call came through after one o'clock in the morning. You had gone back to your digs for the night. You said you were asleep. Would it be normal to respond to that kind of summons from someone who you had known for less than a week?'

Charles didn't like all this harping on the word 'normal'. He felt he was being edged into a position where all of his behaviour might become classed as abnormal. 'I liked Kenny,' he replied rather feebly. 'And he was away from home in a foreign country. So he probably didn't have many other people to ring. I thought if he said he needed help then he probably did need help. And the fact that when I found him he'd been shot through the head suggested that he really did need help.'

This was greeted by a long silence from Detective Inspector Malik and Charles wondered whether he'd been foolish to add the last sentence. But finally she said, 'Yes, you may have a point. So when he called you, how did Mr Polizzi sound?'

'He sounded a bit drunk.'

'Panicky?'

'I'd say "urgent" rather than "panicky".'

'He didn't sound like a man who was actually being threatened by a gun at that moment?'

'No.'

'You may think that's a pointless question I've just asked, Mr Paris, but it could have been useful in establishing the exact time of Mr Polizzi's death.'

'I understand that.'

'The fact that you met Mr Polizzi in a pub where he had evidently been drinking is also interesting to us.' Charles didn't say anything; he'd wait for her to tell him why it was interesting. 'Because Mr Polizzi had made a considerable number of public statements about how he had beaten his addiction to alcohol. He'd even apparently reiterated the fact in a recent interview on British television . . .' She looked down at the iPad. 'On *The Johnny Martin Show*. So inevitably we ask ourselves what it was that made him break his vow of sobriety.'

'I'd been wondering the same thing.'

'And coming to any conclusions?'

'No. I have spoken to Kenny Polizzi's wife, Lilith Greenstone, about that very subject.'

'Yes, we know you have spoken to her, Mr Paris.'

The inspector's words weren't said in a chilling manner, but chilling was the effect they had on Charles. Yes, of course, the uniformed copper in the foyer must've noted his arrival and departure from the Grand Hotel. He wondered how much else they knew. Surely they wouldn't have bugged the Debussy Suite? Would they?

He found himself faffing around for what to say next rather in the way he'd done when playing the guilty husband in a terrible farce called *Don't Get Your Knockers in a Twist*. ('Charles Paris's character died of a heart attack towards the end of Act One – a merciful release to all concerned.' *Malvern Gazette*.)

'Yes, well, I, er . . . Lilith Greenstone's view was that, though their discussion was acrimonious . . . you know, about the final terms for settlement of their divorce . . . that she was still surprised that that should have knocked him off the wagon in such a . . . er, well . . . spectacular style.'

Detective Inspector Malik nodded. 'Yes, that confirms what she said to us. And you don't know of any other meeting Mr Polizzi might have arranged after he'd left Ms Greenstone?'

'No, I don't.'

'But you can see how useful it would be for us to establish the precise sequence of events, what Mr Polizzi actually did, where he went and with whom, that evening?'

'Of course.'

Another silence from Detective Inspector Malik. Then, 'Did Ms Greenstone talk to you about her husband's need for drugs?'

'She did say that when he'd previously taken up drinking again he'd pretty quickly felt an appetite for coke.'

Another confirmatory nod.

'Did Mr Polizzi mention drugs to you, either in his last phone call or at any other time?'

'Not in the phone call, but when we were in the Sea Dog earlier in the evening he asked me if I did drugs. Maybe he thought I could find a supply route for him.'

'And?'

'I had to disappoint him. I'm afraid I've never managed to do drugs successfully.'

This half-joke was greeted by a frozen stare from Detective Inspector Malik. 'Did Mr Polizzi suggest to you that he might have some alternative supply?'

Charles was in a quandary. He couldn't forget Kenny's mention of 'synchronicity' when Lefty Rubenstein rang just after their conversation about drugs. Or the implication in Kenny's responses that the lawyer had successfully sourced something for him. He also remembered Lilith's reference to Lefty frequently obtaining drugs for his employer. But something in Charles rebelled against the idea of landing anyone so firmly in the shit. The police could do their own investigations into the activities of Lefty Rubenstein. He wasn't going to help them. So he answered a negative to Malik's question.

'If we could move on to another matter, Mr Paris . . .'

'Sure.'

'I gather that Mr Polizzi's death has resulted in you taking over his part?'

'Yes. I am now playing Baron Hardup.'

'Is it a part you have always wanted to play, Mr Paris?'

'It's a fun part – one I have played before, actually – but if you're suggesting that my desire to take over the role was strong enough for me to have shot Kenny Polizzi in cold blood . . .'

She did even crack a smile at that. 'I'm sorry, but it's the kind of question I have to ask. Goes with the job.'

'Of course.'

'Did you know that Mr Polizzi had a gun in his possession, Mr Paris?'

Another tricky one, for which a truthful answer could once again implicate Lefty Rubenstein. Charles decided, having backed the lawyer so far, he should continue on the course he'd set himself. 'I didn't know for sure, but Kenny did keep talking about guns. He was a great supporter of the gun lobby at home in the States. He frequently said he felt naked without a gun, so I wouldn't be surprised if he had turned out to be carrying one.'

'But you didn't see him with one?'

Charles's instinctive reaction to protect Lefty was leading him into ever-deeper waters. Still, his vision of the handover of the gun to Kenny outside the pub had been at best blurred. He denied having seen Kenny with a gun. Then, thinking illogically that the gun itself might betray his lie, he asked, 'Has the murder weapon been found, Inspector?'

'No. The assumption must be that the murderer threw it into the sea. Which means it may get washed up somewhere . . . or it may not.'

'Will you be sending divers down to look for it?'

'Perhaps. Though, with the tides being as they are in Eastbourne, I think it could be something of a wild-goose chase. Probably better for us to focus our resources in more fruitful areas.'

'I can see that,' said Charles, feeling obscurely relieved that the gun hadn't been found, as if that would somehow make the police less likely to know he hadn't been telling the truth.

'One further thing, Mr Paris . . .' said Detective Inspector Malik, 'and then we can leave you to enjoy the rest of your Sunday.'

'Yes?'

'We've been in touch with most of the acting company for *Cinderella* – the company stage manager gave us a copy of her contact sheets, and we've spoken to nearly all of them. A few haven't returned our calls on their mobiles and haven't been contactable at their digs . . .'

'That's really no surprise, Inspector. Today, Sunday, is the only scheduled day off in our rehearsal schedule and, what with Eastbourne being relatively near to London, a lot of the company will have gone back home as soon as they heard that yesterday's rehearsal schedule had been cancelled.'

'Thank you for telling us that, Mr Paris. It's very helpful.' Detective Inspector Malik keyed in a note. 'There's one member of the company we are very keen to contact, though. Her name is . . .' she consulted her iPad '. . . Jasmine del Rio. You know her?'

'Yes, of course. I know everyone in the company. Not well, but I know her.'

'But you haven't had any contact with her since Mr Polizzi's murder?'

'No,' replied Charles Paris.

Detective Inspector Malik had said he was free 'to enjoy the rest of his Sunday', but Charles wasn't sure how best to do that. Events of the previous twenty-four hours had left him understandably confused and it took him some time to untangle his emotions and work out the optimum way of spending 'the rest of his Sunday'.

On previous mornings after bedding a new woman, he might have considered a grateful phone call to her, even a suggestion of another tryst. A boozy Sunday lunch together in some relaxed, ungastrified pub, followed by a return visit to her hotel room . . .? But somehow he knew that would be inappropriate for Lilith Greenstone.

Probably a better option would be to stock up with Sunday papers and enjoy the relaxed, ungastrified pub experience on his own. He looked at his watch. Pubs wouldn't open for another hour. And, to keep him going till then, there was a welcoming half-bottle of Bell's back at his digs.

In fact he didn't make it back there. While he was in a convenience store buying a *Sunday Times* and a *Telegraph* (Charles worried he was getting right wing in his old age, but he did find the *Observer* rather smug), his mobile rang.

'Hello. Charles?' A female voice. Pure cockney.

'Sorry, who is this?'

'It's Kitty Woo . . . you know, the dancer from—'

'Of course I know who you are. What can I do for you?'

'Well, I just wondered if you'd heard anything from Jasmine . . . you know, Jasmine del Rio who—'

'Yes, of course I know.' Second time he'd been asked the same question that morning. 'No, I'm afraid I haven't. Not since we finished rehearsal on Friday.'

'Oh.' The girl sounded so desolated that Charles suggested they should meet up for a drink. A pub lunch, maybe . . .?

She sounded almost pathetically pleased by the suggestion. 'That'd be great, Charles. So long as we sit outside.'

'Oh. Why's that?'

'So that I can smoke.'

ELEVEN

CINDERELLA: Oh, I'm so lonely. Pushed and shoved
By my two sisters, I'll never be loved.

The weak early December sun didn't do any of the things that the sun is supposed to do, like provide warmth, and Charles was glad of the ancient duffel coat he had once again wrapped himself in. Kitty Woo, in a short leather jacket and even shorter leather skirt, seemed impervious to the weather. She said at first she didn't want anything alcoholic but changed her mind and had a vodka tonic. She said she wasn't hungry either, but decided to have a prawn sandwich. Charles started with a pint of Harvey's by way of rehydration (he'd move on to the red wine later) and ordered the full roast beef and Yorkshire pudding Sunday lunch.

There was no reticence about Kitty Woo. As Charles had observed during rehearsal breaks, she and Jasmine del Rio had talked incessantly to each other and the dancer proved herself just as proficient at monologue as duologue. She was one of those people who seemed to be distressed if a nanosecond of silence was allowed to go unfilled.

'Thing is about me and Jazzy,' she said, 'we've been mates for ever. We met when we was both at Italia Conti – you know?' Charles nodded. He was familiar with the children's drama school and over his career had met quite a few of its products. 'And we've kind of joined up together whenever we could – work and boyfriends permitting. There've been some big breaks obviously, like when she was working in the States for a couple of years, but whenever we see each other again, it's like we can pick up the conversation straight away – you know, like one of us has only just walked out the room for like a couple of minutes. So it was like really good news when we found out we was both working on this *Cinderella*, because we have been in the same shows over the years but not that often . . . and we've both worked with Bix before because he, sort of, likes to work with people he knows, but in fact this was the first time Jazzy and me was in one of his shows together. And that's great, 'cause we drove down here in Jazzy's Figaro and—'

'Sorry, what's a Figaro?'

'Little car. Really cute. Looks like a kid's toy . . . except of course it's full size. Jazzy's is Mint Green. We drove down here in it together – really like a girls' adventure – we're sharing these really nice digs and we was looking forward to spending some time together . . . you know, specially like over Christmas, because neither of us have got anything in the way of family – well, not family we're speaking to, anyway, and we're both between boyfriends, so, you know, it was like really good.'

A momentary pause for Kitty to take in a gulp of air gave Charles the opportunity to ask, 'But you haven't seen her since Friday?'

'No, like, we finished rehearsals and I was going to cook that evening for us, like full Chinese – not that muck you get in Chinese restaurants but real Chinese like my grandmother used to cook. And Jazzy said fine, there was something she'd got to do but she'd be back nine at the latest, so she drove off in the Figaro, and I got all the stuff ready, because a lot of Chinese food you have to cook really quick, like, and I just waited. And, anyway, Jazzy never turned up.'

'No message from her?'

'Had a text about nine saying she was running a bit late, but that was it. Which is odd, because Jazzy's like Queen of the Texts. If she's not actually with me, then she's like texting me all the time. Never without the latest iPhone and it's like an extension to her hand she uses it so much. Always texting and scribbling down stuff on the little Notes app. God knows how she ever survived before they invented the iPhone. Which is why it's so strange that I haven't heard anything more from her since that text on Friday.' Kitty sounded on the edge of tears.

'Do the police know this – about the text you had?' asked Charles.

For the first time in their conversation Kitty looked a little suspicious. 'Why do you ask that?'

'Because I've just been talking to Detective Inspector Malik and she asked me if I'd seen Jasmine.'

'Oh. Right. Well, yes, they did ask me, and I didn't want to tell them Jazzy was missing.'

'Why not?'

'My dad always told me never to tell the police anything you don't need to tell them. One of the few useful pieces of advice he ever give me. This was before he pissed off with some tart when I was, like, nine.'

'Was your father Chinese?' asked Charles.

'God, no. British through and through. Eastender and a total racist.'

'That must've been, er . . . interesting, with him married to your mother.'

'No, they was never married. Did live together for a few years. But it didn't make for domestic harmony, no. Not much fun being around the house when your dad keeps calling your mum a "slit-eyed Chink" – specially since I was nearly as "slit-eyed" as she was, like. No, not easy round our place. Bloody relief when the old bugger did piss off, actually.'

'And you and your mother?'

'Always at each other's throats . . . for different reasons. She was never interested in me. Me being half-English meant I was neither one thing nor the other so far as she was concerned. My mum was racist too in her way. Went back to Hong Kong . . . ooh, over ten years ago now. Haven't heard from her since. Only good thing I ever got from her was the knowledge of how to cook Chinese – and most of that came from my gran, but she died way back.'

Charles realized what Kitty had meant about having no family she was speaking to. He was also aware of how dependent someone in her isolated position would be on her friends, and the level of upset that Jasmine del Rio's disappearance must have caused her. It was hard to read the emotions in the girl's black eyes, but she was clearly in a bad state. Jasmine meant a lot to her.

He moved the conversation back to Kitty's interview with the police. 'But you didn't tell the cops a lie, did you, and say that you'd seen Jasmine after the end of rehearsals on Friday?'

'No, no. I just made it sound like it was no big deal . . . you know, like she was always pissing off somewhere in the Figaro and picking up men and I wasn't at all worried about her not coming back.'

The arrival of their lunches brought a natural break in proceedings. The waitress, dressed in thin black shirt and trousers, clearly thought that anyone who sat outside on a day like that was certifiable.

'So the big question really is,' asked Charles, after he'd ordered another vodka tonic and a large Merlot from the waitress, 'what was this "thing" Jasmine said she'd got to do on Friday evening before coming back for your Chinese banquet?'

'Yes,' Kitty agreed. 'Mind you, I didn't tell the police that I was expecting her back.'

'No, of course not. So, Kitty, do you have any idea where Jasmine went that evening?'

The black eyes looked puzzled as she shook her head back and forth. 'No, I don't. I just know she went in the car. But there'd been something odd with her since she arrived in Eastbourne.'

'Odd? Like how?'

'She was kind of tense. I mean, she had just come through a particularly nasty break-up with some bloke who'd seemed to tick all the boxes and then turned out to be a bastard like every other man.' She allowed herself a little grin. 'No offence.'

He grinned back. 'None taken.'

'And it was one of these situations where they'd actually moved in together and she'd lent him money for some business project he was supposed to be setting up. And of course that was never going to work out, was it? So Jazzy didn't only end up with a big emotional slap in the face, she lost all her savings too.'

'I apologize on behalf of my gender,' said Charles.

'Apology bloody rejected,' said Kitty with another pale grin. She was only toying with her prawn sandwich and lighting the next cigarette from the stub of the last one. 'Anyway, Jazzy was very worried about money – you know, she'd been renting in London and she ended that when she came down here, so she, like, hadn't got a place to call her own. End of the *Cinderella* run and she'll be homeless, which, OK, has happened to her before, but it's never going to be a barrel of laughs, is it? Jazzy was even talking about having to sell the Figaro, and that's like her proudest possession. And I'd lent her some money because I'm quite flush at the moment, and she didn't like being in debt to me and kept saying she'd be able to pay me back soon. I said it wasn't a big deal, but it upset her. So Jazzy was in a bad way.'

'And you don't think it's just a reaction to the ending of the relationship?'

'That could be a big part of it, but I think there's more.'

'Any idea what?'

Kitty shook her head ruefully. 'She seemed kind of twitchy, nervous before going to rehearsals, which is just so unlike Jazzy. She's seen everything in the business, done everything. Worked with bastard choreographers, worked with groping directors, worked with impossible divas. Nothing fazes Jazzy. But there was something about the *Cinderella* company that unsettled her.'

'Some*thing* or some*one*?'

'More likely someone.'

'An ex?'

'Maybe. But looking through the personnel I can't think who it's likely to be.'

'No. Did she mention whether anyone in the company had come on to her since she'd been down here?'

'Well, yes, there's always a bit of that early in rehearsals. Not from the male dancers, obviously – not their scene at all – but there's usually some Jack the Lad among the actors who tries it on. A few of them chatted me up, but pretty quickly saw they weren't going to get anywhere.'

'And did the same thing happen with Jasmine?'

'Yes, of course. Occupational hazard in our line of business.'

'And did things go further with Jasmine and anyone in the cast?'

'No. She might have had a drink with someone, but nothing more. I told you, she's currently as pissed off with the male of the species as I am.'

'Thank you,' said Charles.

They were silent for a moment. He mopped up the last of his gravy with the last of his roast potatoes. The Sunday lunch had been surprisingly good, a defence against the cold wind from the sea that somehow found its way into every open cranny of his ancient duffel coat. Kitty Woo, in her skimpy leathers, still seemed impervious to the climatic conditions. Then he asked, 'Does the name Marybeth Docker mean anything to you?'

Kitty shook her head in bewilderment. She'd clearly never heard it before in her life.

'Because I think that's what Jasmine del Rio may have called herself when she was in the States.'

Kitty shrugged. 'Possible. She never mentioned it to me.'

'Do you know much about the time when she went over there?'

'Not a lot. As I say, we were both, like, at Italia Conti, and suddenly Jazzy announces she's, like, going to try her luck in the States. I was pretty gobsmacked, I can tell you, because we was the same age, and I was far too young to think about doing something like that. Needless to say there was a man involved. There was always a man involved with Jazzy. Well, and sometimes a woman.'

'Oh?'

'Jazzy has had the odd lesbian fling.' She seemed to read something in Charles's expression. 'Not with me, for God's sake. We're just mates. But Jazzy's a great believer in love – in spite of the evidence that it always goes wrong for her – and she's not that bothered who the love comes from. Gender's a detail for her. There was a woman director called Laura she shacked up with for six months or so, a good while back. I think she found it rather restful, after all the crap she'd had to put up with from men. Didn't last, though. When it comes to relationships there's a bit of a kamikaze streak in Jazzy. She was soon two-timing Laura with another bloody man.'

'And what about the man she went to the States with?'

'He was American – and a kind of standard-issue bullshitter. Claimed to be a big producer over there, though I reckon that was just a ploy to get inside the knickers of as many actresses and dancers as he could. And Jazzy had matured young, always looked a good three or four years older than her real age.'

'That's a point, though. How could she get into the States if she was only a kid? She didn't presumably go with her parents or—'

'No, no, this guy she was with was a real fixer. He organized a false passport for her, which said she was eighteen. He was so obviously a crook and a bastard, but she couldn't see it. He'd said he'd take her to the States and launch her career over there – and she believed him. Untold fortunes awaited them there, he said. All he asked her to do was find the money for both their air fares.'

'*Both* their air fares?'

'Yes, I'm afraid, like I say, there is a pattern in Jazzy's relationship with men. In spite of playing tough all the time she's a complete sucker for anything a man tells her – and she was even more so back then. So, soon as they're safely in LA, the so-called producer, her so-called boyfriend, so-called fiancé even, suddenly vanishes off the scene. Leaving Jazzy on her own, trying to find work in one of the most competitive marketplaces in the entire world.'

'Do you know what happened to her?'

A shake of the head. 'Not in detail. She doesn't like to talk about it. I think it was bloody tough, but she did get work eventually. She's a grafter, Jazzy. Can always sort things out in every area of her life.'

'Except men.'

'Except men.'

'Kitty, did she ever tell you she had met Kenny Polizzi before?'

'No. Never mentioned a thing about him. Why, did she meet him?'

'She implied that she had.' And Charles recapitulated the encounter he'd witnessed between the two of them during the Thursday rehearsal break. 'And she said that when they'd met previously she was called Marybeth Docker. And he looked very shocked by that.'

'What did he say?'

'Rehearsal started again. He didn't have time to say anything.'

Kitty looked puzzled and a little shaken by what Charles had told her. 'So if there was a connection between Jazzy and Kenny Polizzi, then maybe she was going to see him on Friday night . . .?'

'It's possible. It's also possible that whatever she said to him had such an effect on him that he started drinking again.'

'How'd do you mean?'

'Kenny fell very spectacularly off the wagon on Friday night.'

'I didn't know that.'

'He'd had a fairly stormy encounter with Lilith Greenstone, his . . . well, she was still technically his wife, but she reckoned that wouldn't have upset him enough to break his pledge. Something else that happened that night, however, shook him up so much that he reached straight for the vodka bottle.'

Kitty looked thoughtful. 'And you think it could have been something to do with Jazzy. What kind of connection could there be between her and Kenny?'

'Well, let's start with the obvious one, shall we?' said Charles. 'Sex. You say Jasmine always looked older than her years. How old was she when she flew to the States with her dodgy producer?'

'Fourteen,' replied Kitty Woo.

TWELVE

BARON HARDUP: I always suffer from paranoia
When I have dealings with a lawyer.

Charles had a lot to think about after he left Kitty. The girl was desperately worried about her friend's disappearance and this gave him a further incentive to find out what, if anything, had happened between Jasmine del Rio and Kenny Polizzi on the Friday evening. He mentally went through the members of the *Cinderella* company to think who might possibly have some relevant information, but drew a blank. The one person he was keen to contact, though, was Lefty Rubenstein. Surely Kenny's factotum must know something about his employer's movements on the Friday night. The end of the phone conversation Charles had heard in the pub suggested that Lefty was sourcing cocaine for him. And if that was the case, then the two of them must have met up that evening.

The trouble was that Charles didn't have any means of contacting the lawyer. He knew Lefty wasn't in the Grand, but didn't know which hotel he was staying in. And Charles had no mobile number for him. For all he knew, after his boss's death Lefty had flown straight back to the States.

Back at his digs, Charles took a long swig of Bell's to act as a *digestif* after his lunch and then sat down to think seriously about the disappearance of Jasmine del Rio.

He was woken once again by the ringing of his mobile. The fact that it was Lilith calling brought him instantly to wakefulness.

'Charles,' she said, efficient, no-nonsense, businesslike, 'I'm flying back to the States on tonight's red eye. I just thought I should tell you we won't be repeating last night's experiment.'

'Oh,' said Charles, understandably deflated.

'You're not what I'm looking for,' she went on, her words not calculated to do much by way of reinflating him. 'But I did just want to tell you that I have very good lawyers.'

'You already told me that. You said they were dealing with the divorce in a way—'

'I'm not talking about the divorce. I'm talking about the possibility of you going to the press about what happened last night.'

'What? You mean you think I'm likely to produce a kiss-and-tell memoir?'

'Someone in my position always has to be wary of that possibility.'

Charles was insulted and let Lilith know he was. 'Look, it's a little diminishing for a man to be told he's an inadequate lover, but—'

'I didn't say you were inadequate, just not what I'm looking for.'

'Well, thank you very much for making that distinction. But what really offends me is that you think I'm the kind of man who would try and sell "My Night of Passion with Lilith Greenstone" stories to the press.'

'I'm sorry, but I have to take precautions against that kind of thing happening. And all I'm saying is that if you ever change your mind about spilling the beans, my lawyers will leave you so shredded and beat up you'll wish you'd never been born.'

'I can assure you,' said Charles with some hauteur, 'that the eventuality you describe will never arise.'

'I'm very glad to hear that, Charles.' Then she added formally, 'It was a kinda pleasure to meet you. We won't meet again.'

'Oh, before you ring off, there is one thing I want from you.'

'Oh?' said Lilith, bridling.

'I'd be grateful if you could give me Lefty Rubenstein's mobile – I mean, cellphone number.'

Lilith could see no reason why that was an illegitimate demand, so she gave Charles the number.

No time like the present. He called Lefty straight away.

And his call was answered straight away. No self-identification, just a cautious 'Hi.'

'Lefty, it's Charles Paris.'

'Oh yeah?'

'I just wanted to say I'm very sorry about what happened to Kenny.'

'Well, that's very gracious and British of you, but it's not really necessary. Kenny's dead, that's all there is. Kinda life he led it was no big surprise.'

'Yes, but there's a lot of discussion in the *Cinderella* company about what might have happened to him.'

'I'm sure there is. There's a lot of discussion in the entire world about what might have happened to him. Kenny Polizzi was an international star. I haven't dared look at your Sunday papers yet. But you should see the number of tweets there've been just this morning.'

Charles did by now know what a 'tweet' was. Something to do with Twitter. But he'd never actually seen one. Although he knew most of his fellow professionals were wedded to it, there had yet to be a meaningful interface between Charles Paris and the social media.

'Well, Lefty, I was wondering if you were clearer than anyone else about what actually happened on Friday night.'

'Why should I be?'

'Last time I saw Kenny alive I was drinking with him in the pub by the theatre. He was asking me about drugs and then the phone rang. He saw who was calling and he said it was synchronicity.'

'So?'

'The phone call was from you.'

'What makes you think that?'

'He called you "Lefty".'

'So maybe Kenny had a lot of friends called Lefty.'

'Maybe, but I'd say it was unlikely.'

'What are you saying, Charles? What's with this "synchronicity"?'

'I think you were ringing Kenny to say you'd managed to find some cocaine for him.'

'Is that what you think?' said Lefty shortly. 'We better meet.'

It wasn't the Grand. Lefty had selected an anonymous modern hotel, a few roads back from the sea front. The bar had as much atmosphere as a bedroom in a private hospital. A premature undecorated Christmas tree did little to cheer the place up. Late on a Sunday afternoon there was no one else there but an older

man and a younger woman, clearly too involved in the complications of their extramarital affair to listen to anyone else's
conversation. Even the barman had to be summoned by ringing
a bell on the counter. Charles Paris ordered a large Bell's, Lefty
Rubenstein had another of his Diet Cokes, drunk straight out of
the bottle.

'So have the police talked to you, Charles?' he asked. He
looked sweaty and uncomfortable, his bulbous body barely
contained by his crumpled suit, the comb-over uneven across his
head.

'Yes. And presumably to you?'

'Of course. I'm Kenny's attorney. Not to mention his agent
and everything else.'

'And did you get any impression of the direction in which the
police's investigations were heading?'

'Surely even British cops wouldn't be stupid enough to let
anyone know that.'

Charles felt duly put down by the response. 'No. You're right.'

'When you rang me on my cell you talked about drugs and
the idea that I might have obtained cocaine for Kenny . . .'

'Yes.'

'You have any reason for thinking I did that?'

'Just what he said about synchronicity.'

'Hm.' Lefty took a moment to assess that response. Then he
asked, 'Did you say anything to the police about this
"synchronicity"?'

Charles was able to reply an honest, 'No.'

'So when you talked to the police drugs weren't mentioned?'

'Yes, they were. Detective Inspector Malik – did you meet
her?'

'Sure I did.'

'She was the one who raised the subject of drugs with me. I
got the impression Lilith Greenstone had told her that Kenny
tended to fancy some cocaine every time he started drinking
again.'

Lefty nodded ruefully. 'That figures. Lilith would have said
that. The bitch.'

'She also,' Charles began cautiously, 'suggested that on occasion you sourced cocaine for Kenny.'

The lawyer looked horrified. 'She said that to the cops?'

'No. Not so far as I know. She said that to me.'

'Ah.' Lefty smiled a crooked smile. 'You been spending a bit of time with the lovely Lilith?' Charles found himself blushing. 'Yeah, that figures. She always liked variety.' Then he became serious. 'Listen, Charles, this situation I'm in is a real shithole. My responsibilities don't stop with Kenny's death. I've managed the guy's image for years, and I reckon that job's just got harder. While he was alive and he did something stupid, we could always limit the damage. Get him to own up, go on some chat show, be all contrition. We could work it out. Protecting his image without him there is going to be one hell of a lot trickier.'

'But why do you need to manage his image now he's dead?'

'Hell, don't you know anything about showbiz, Charles? Kenny Polizzi is still one hell of a big star. The media'll be all over the story. Possibly dead he'll be a bigger star than ever. Remember the line about Elvis – dying was "a good career move". You see the same thing with Michael Jackson. *The Dwight House* is still being repeated round the world. There's a lot invested in seeing that the image of Kenny Polizzi doesn't get tarnished.'

'Why does it matter so much to you, Lefty?'

'It matters so much to me,' he replied, 'because I'm on a percentage of everything that comes in. I may not be that sentimental about people, but I'm sure as hell sentimental about money.'

Lefty swallowed down the last of his Diet Coke, jumped up to the bar and banged on the bell to be supplied with another one. Just to be sociable, Charles ordered a second large Bell's.

While the barman was getting their drinks, Charles noticed that the woman of the extramarital couple was crying. The man's guilt must have been clicking in, now he was preparing to go back home to his wife and children. The lie about 'a conference in Eastbourne' felt pretty shabby to him now. Satiated with sex, he had no doubt just told the girl the thing had to end (as he no doubt would on many more occasions). To Charles the whole scenario had an uncomfortable familiarity.

Lefty once again sat down opposite him. 'Listen, keep it the way it is with the cops. If they ask you more about Kenny and drugs, act dumb. You know nothing. And if they should happen to ask you if you'd ever heard of me procuring coke for Kenny, you know even less. Got that?'

'Sure thing,' said Charles, taking on the actor's habit of beginning to talk like the person he was with. 'But there are things about Friday night I still want to know.'

The lawyer's eyes narrowed. 'Yeah? Like what?'

'You did meet up with Kenny, didn't you?'

'Why should I tell you whether I did or not?'

He didn't like doing it, but Charles was so intrigued by the puzzle of Kenny Polizzi's murder that he said, 'To ensure I don't forget what you just told me and happen to mention to Detective Inspector Malik that you have on occasion sourced coke for him.'

He'd feared this would prompt an outburst, but in fact Lefty took it very calmly. Maybe, as a lawyer, he was used to negotiation. He was used to a world where information was just another bargaining counter.

'OK.' He nodded. 'That's your pitch. And you put me in the kind of bind – which I'm sure was exactly what you intended to do. If I don't tell you more about Friday night, you're threatening to spill the beans to Malik about me sourcing coke for Kenny. If I do tell you, you then have more beans to spill, should you change your mind about staying shtum.'

'I won't.'

'Your word is your bond? Very British, Charles Paris. Hm.' Lefty was silent for a moment. He took a long swig from his Diet Coke and swept his sweaty comb-over back across his head. 'As it happens, I am inclined to tell you more, and that's for one simple reason.'

'What?'

'Because I'm as keen as you are to find out what actually happened to Kenny on Friday evening.'

'Who killed him, you mean?'

'Exactly that. If the two of us pool our information, maybe we have a better chance of reaching a solution.'

Charles liked the way the conversation was heading. He already had the feeling that he'd embarked on an investigation. To have Lefty Rubenstein, with all his knowledge of Kenny Polizzi's past history, on his side would be a considerable bonus.

'Sounds good to me, Lefty. If you answer a few questions for me I'll tell you anything I know – though I'm afraid that probably isn't much.'

'You say that, Charles, but you were the one who actually found Kenny's body.'

'Yes, but I don't know if I was the first person to find it.'

'Well, let's assume for the time being that you were. So how long would you say it took from you getting the call from Kenny's cell and arriving at the pier?'

'Half an hour tops. I'd have been there quicker if I hadn't forgotten my coat and gone back to the digs to get it. I still feel guilty about that.'

'Don't think about it. Guilt is one of the most wasteful of all human emotions.' Given its source, Charles found this an unexpectedly philosophical observation. 'And you didn't see anyone other than Kenny when you got under the pier?'

'No.'

'No one hurrying away?'

Charles shook his head. 'I mean, obviously I had no suspicions at the time, so it's not as if I was looking out for anyone, but my recollection is of not seeing a soul, even thinking to myself what a sedate place Eastbourne was, with all its inhabitants tucked up in bed by two o'clock in the morning.'

Lefty nodded thoughtfully. 'And you saw no sign of the murder weapon?'

'No. Detective Inspector Malik was of the view that it had probably been thrown into the sea, and that the chances of recovering it were minimal.'

'Oh?'

'Something to do with the tides round Eastbourne, I don't know.' Another nod from the lawyer. 'Lefty, I have to ask you . . . did you find cocaine for Kenny that evening?'

'Yes, I did.'

'How did you know where to look?'

'Kind of thing you pick up if you're raised on the back streets of LA.'

'You found the stuff very quickly. Presumably you only started looking after Kenny had started drinking and contacted you?'

'Yes, but I'd done my research beforehand. You'd be amazed at the network of contacts lawyers have. In LA, of course, I deal through respectable sources. Getting drugs there is like any other service. You pay the right amount of money, you get the right amount of discretion. Here I had to take more risks. New place, you don't know quite who you'll be dealing with. But my contacts came up with the goods. Got me a few useful names and numbers here in Eastbourne. Individuals, pubs they might frequent, that kinda stuff.'

'Why did you do that, Lefty? Why did you think you'd need drugs here?'

'Because I'd seen Kenny fall off the wagon many times before. And this was the longest time he'd been sober for a while. I knew it couldn't last. And I always like to be prepared for every eventuality.'

Charles was once again surprised at the breadth of the job description for acting as Kenny Polizzi's lawyer and agent. 'And would you be prepared,' he asked, 'to let me have those contact details?'

'I thought you said you'd never done drugs? Strange time of life to change something like that.'

'No, I don't want the drugs for myself. I just thought it might be useful for me to know for the next stage of our investigation.'

Lefty didn't look convinced. 'I got all the information we need about that. No need for you to start poking a stick in a hornets' nest. Drug trade here in Eastbourne – like everywhere else in the world – involves some seriously unwholesome characters.'

'OK,' said Charles lightly, reminding himself that he and Lefty had just agreed to work on the investigation together. If that partnership worked out, then fine. If not, Charles might have to start exploring the Eastbourne drug trade on his own.

There was a sudden commotion the other side of the bar. The weeping girl pushed her chair back and ran out of the room. The man looked embarrassed with relief. He rang for the barman and ordered a double gin and tonic. And prepared himself for a virtuous return to the wife who'd never known of the other woman's existence.

'Lefty, does the name Marybeth Docker mean anything to you?'

Suspicion returned to the dark eyes. 'In what context?'

'In the context of Kenny Polizzi. In the context of a girl he might have met some years back in LA?'

'Kenny met a lot of girls back in LA.'

'He might have had a sexual relationship with this Marybeth Docker.'

'Kenny had sexual relationships with a lot of girls back in LA.'

'This one is in the *Cinderella* company. Now under the name of Jasmine del Rio.'

Lefty Rubenstein shook his head. 'Neither name means anything to me.'

'Because I was wondering whether Jasmine offered some kind of threat to Kenny.' And Charles described the encounter between the two of them that he'd witnessed in the rehearsal room.

But his narrative only prompted another shake of the head. 'Though I may be like Kenny's nursemaid, I don't have a record of every woman he screwed. Particularly not if we're going back to before the *Dwight House* days.'

'Oh well, if you do hear anything about a woman with either of those names, let me know.'

'Sure will.' Lefty seemed more relaxed as he took another long swig from his bottle. That finished the contents, so he rang the bell on the bar for a refill. Still being sociable, Charles ordered another large Bell's.

The other drinker in the bar downed the remains of his gin and tonic and walked out, back to his unsuspecting wife with a step that was almost jaunty.

'How long are you going to stay in England?' asked Charles once they were again seated.

'A little while yet, I think. Need to be near the police investigation, be one of the first to know when there's any progress. My staff back in LA can handle the US media. Besides, given the scale of Kenny's name, a lot of the papers and TV companies will probably be sending their news teams over here – if they haven't arrived already. I need to be around here to manage how they report the story.'

'I can see that.'

Lefty looked at his watch. 'I gotta get back up to my room. Lotta emails to do.'

'Well, it's been good to see you.' Charles reached across the table to shake the lawyer's hand. 'And we're agreed – any useful information either of us gets on the investigation – we share it.'

'Sure thing,' said Lefty.

Charles held on to the man's hand. 'And I think that should include you telling me who the contact was in Eastbourne through whom you got the cocaine for Kenny.'

There was only a token remonstrance before Lefty gave in. He gave the name of a pub and the name of a man to ask for there.

'But be careful, Charles,' was his parting shot. 'People who deal drugs are rarely the nice guys.'

THIRTEEN

BUTTONS: But will you love me in the end?
CINDERELLA: No, but I'll always be your friend.

There were two pieces of news at the start of rehearsals on the Monday morning. One was about recasting. The elevation of Charles Paris to the role of Baron Hardup had left the production one Broker's Man short. And following the bizarre process that goes under the name of 'celebrity casting' in pantomimes, it had been decided that Mick 'The Cobra' Mesquito should be paired up with another boxer.

During his career in the ring he had had an ongoing rivalry (in small part genuine, in large part puffed up by the media) with a fellow welterweight called Garry 'Bomber' Brawn. They had had two memorable fights ('memorable' being a relative term since they were both British and there have never been any truly memorable boxing matches that didn't involve Americans). In the first the 'Bomber' had taken Mesquito's British Welterweight title, in the second the 'Cobra' had regained it. Both fights had been uninspiring contests with the fighters doing a lot of holding and leaning against each other, shuffling round the ring like superannuated ballroom dancers. And both had been won on a split points decision.

But for some reason – perhaps lack of competition or rose-tinted recollection – they had gone down in the British sporting memory as epic encounters. So the introduction of Garry 'Bomber' Brawn into the cast of *Cinderella* was reckoned to be something of a publicity coup (not that after the murder of Kenny Polizzi the production really needed any more publicity).

The casting of a second boxer also cheered Bix Rogers enormously. Ever since he'd seen *Rocky* he'd wanted to choreograph a boxing match, and finally his opportunity had arrived. The interpolation of another irrelevance of course wreaked further havoc with *Cinderella*'s plot, but the director had long since stopped caring about that. And Danny Fitz was once again driven to silent fury by the elbowing of another of his traditional pantomime routines.

The other piece of news on that Monday morning's rehearsal was that Jasmine del Rio had disappeared.

At the lunch break Charles found Kitty Woo, predictably enough standing in the cold outside St Asaph's Church Halls, puffing away at a cigarette as desperately as if it were her oxygen supply at the top of Everest.

'Presumably you haven't heard any more from Jasmine?'

The dancer shook her head. The lids around her black eyes were puffy. She'd been crying.

'And you haven't remembered anything about her time as Marybeth Docker?'

'Like I said before, she never mentioned the name.'

'I was just thinking, Kitty, you said you had a text from Jasmine on Friday evening about nine . . .?'

'Yes. It said she was a bit delayed.'

'Anything else?'

By way of answer Kitty whipped out her mobile and, with that young person's dexterity that never failed to amaze Charles, clicked icons to produce the relevant text.

'*Running a bit late. Looking forward to the Chinese – and will pay you back, promise. X J.*'

'What did she mean about paying you back?'

'I guessed she meant she'd cook for me another night.'

'Sure it wasn't money? You said she'd borrowed some from you.'

'Yes, I suppose it might have been that. I didn't really think about it.'

'But if that's what she meant, it might imply that she was going to get some money on the Friday night.'

'Could do.' Kitty sounded listless. Her level of hope was low, she was close to despair.

'Hm.' Charles looked pityingly at the girl. 'And otherwise . . . I assume you've heard nothing?'

'Not from Jazzy, no.'

'But you have heard from someone else?' he asked keenly.

'Text from Laura Hahn.' The name meant nothing to Charles.

'Woman Jazzy lived with for a while. Theatre director. I'm sure I mentioned her.'

'Yes, you did, but I don't think you told me her surname.'

'Ah, right. No, I probably didn't. Anyway, Laura's heard about Jazzy being missing and she's dead worried. I think she's probably still in love with her a bit. She's coming down here from London this afternoon.'

'To look for Jasmine?'

'Yes, though I don't know that she'll have any more success finding her than we have.'

'No.'

'Actually it might make sense, Charles, if you met her too.'

'Oh?'

'Well, you can talk to Laura about the possible Kenny Polizzi connection. She might know something.'

'Yes, I suppose she might. If they lived together. Must've talked about all kinds of things, possibly including Jasmine's time as Marybeth Docker.'

'Mm. You haven't heard any more from the police, have you, Charles?'

He shook his head. 'Why should I have?'

'Well, I was just thinking, now Jazzy hasn't turned up to rehearsals, it's kind of like she's officially missing. The police will be wanting to find out more about her movements on Friday. I wouldn't be surprised if I get another call from them.' She closed her eyes and clenched her hands tightly together, almost as if she was praying. 'Oh, I hope to God nothing's happened to her.'

'Well, if she's disappeared, there must be a reason.'

'She's been abducted.'

'Not necessarily.'

'Why not? Why else would she suddenly disappear off the face of the earth?'

'To escape.'

'Escape from what?'

'Kitty, if there was some past history between Jasmine and

Kenny, then she might have confronted him about it. Kenny might have pulled out a gun . . .'

'And shot her?'

'Jasmine's body hasn't been found.'

'But Kenny's body has been.'

'Exactly.'

'Charles, are you suggesting that it was Jazzy who shot him?'

'Well, it's a possibility.'

Laura Hahn was tall and elegant in grey trousers and cream silk shirt under a dark blue knitted jacket. Her shoulder-length hair was dyed a bright scarlet which made no attempt to ape anything in nature. As with most of the gay people of Charles's acquaintance, if the subject hadn't come up he would never have guessed her sexual orientation.

She had a lot of poise and, although she was clearly worried about Jasmine, she seemed to be completely in control of her emotions. Charles thought she would probably be a very good director. She had an air of calm competence. He and other actors would relax under her authority.

The three of them met later that afternoon in a coffee shop, which felt a bit odd to Charles. He'd nothing against coffee, but not having an alcoholic drink after rehearsal didn't seem quite natural. He had hardly ever been in a coffee shop. The Starbucks revolution had passed him by. There had always been a pub close enough for him not to seek out any teetotal alternative.

The women both ordered sticky cakes too, which again felt strange. He'd never had much of a taste for sweet things, so he stuck to a double espresso. The smell brought back to him a dreadful farce set in a restaurant in which he'd played an Italian waiter. ('Charles Paris's accent kept slipping like a recalcitrant bra-strap.' *Teesside Evening Gazette.*)

Kitty quickly brought Laura up to date with the last contact she and Charles had had with Jasmine. She didn't mention the recent suggestion that the dance captain might have murdered Kenny. 'Have you heard anything from her more recently?'

Laura shook her head with something like wistfulness. 'No,

since she moved out, contact with Jasmine has been intermittent at best.' Charles was interested to hear the use of her full name. Clearly 'Jazzy' was something just Kitty Woo used. 'I had a text from her saying she'd been dumped by the latest man and got this *Cinderella* job, but that's probably three weeks back. I couldn't resist coming down here, though. There's been so much in the press about the murder. I've just got a bad feeling that something terrible's happened to Jasmine.'

'Yes, I feel that too,' said Kitty.

Charles felt he ought to say something calming. 'We don't know it's something terrible. She may have had reasons of her own to make herself scarce.'

'Rather odd, though, happening at the same time as the murder,' said Laura. 'Feels like the two things must be connected.'

'I know what you mean. And of course her car's missing too. At least I assume it is, Kitty?'

'Yes, haven't seen the Figaro since she went off in it on Friday.'

'But you did tell the police about it?' Charles wasn't sure how far the dancer's bloody-minded non-cooperation with the authorities would go.

'Oh yes, they've got the registration number and what-have-you.'

'Maybe they've already found it,' suggested Charles.

'If they have they're hardly likely to tell us, are they?'

'No. Maybe they'll announce something in one of their press conferences.'

'Maybe.' Kitty still sounded very dispirited.

Charles turned his attention to Laura Hahn. 'Actually, there is one thing I'd like to ask you, since you clearly know Jasmine del Rio pretty well.'

'I thought I did,' came the embittered reply.

'Did she ever talk to you about having used the name Marybeth Docker?'

The response was immediate. 'Yes, that was what Jasmine called herself when she was in the States, trying to make a career out there. Way back, when she was just in her teens.'

'Did she talk to you much about that period?' asked Charles.

'Not a lot. I don't think it was one of the happier times of her life.'

'Did she ever say why she changed her name?'

'I think it was probably to sound more American. Trying to get work out in LA for an unknown was pretty hard. For an unknown Brit it was even harder. I think that must've been when she picked up that mid-Atlantic accent she never really got rid of.' Laura spoke with fond nostalgia. Clearly the feelings she had for her ex-lover remained strong.

Charles asked, 'Might her reinvention of herself in the States also have had something to do with her age?'

'You're probably right. From what she told me, she was only fourteen when she went out there. So yes, that could be another reason for her obscuring her origins.'

'Did she talk to you about any relationships she had while she was out there?'

'Sexual relationships?'

'Yes.'

'Only in pretty general terms. I think there were plenty of predatory men round LA at the time. So what else is new? There are predatory men around everywhere all the time. But I got the impression from Jasmine that some of the dancing jobs she got involved her putting in some work on the casting couch.'

'That doesn't still happen, does it?' asked Kitty, sounding surprisingly shocked by the idea. 'It's never happened to me.'

'Then you've been unusually fortunate. The casting couch has always happened,' Laura replied. 'Even in these right-on, politically correct days it still happens. Power goes to men's heads – and not just their heads. But, anyway, in Jasmine's case we are talking twelve, fifteen years ago. Gender politics hadn't advanced so far back then.'

'Did she mention any names?' asked Charles. 'You know, of the men she supplied sexual favours to?'

'No. I didn't get the impression any of them were particularly memorable. She just did what she needed to do to get the job. When it came to sex, Jasmine always did have a very pragmatic side to her,' Laura concluded ruefully.

'And she didn't mention the name of Kenny Polizzi?' The director shook her head. 'Or any other big-name star?'

Another shake of the head. 'Anyway, would Kenny Polizzi have been a big star back then? I thought he came from more or less total obscurity to star in *The Dwight House*.'

'You could be right.' Charles sighed with frustration and looked at the swirl of brown in the bottom of his espresso cup. Now he really did need a proper drink. 'If only we could find Jasmine and ask her.'

'That is the problem, yes.' Laura looked desperately sad for a moment before she quickly covered up the feeling. She looked at Kitty. 'It's unlike her just to take off in the middle of a job, isn't it?'

'She'd never do that. She's got, like, this really strong work ethic. Once she'd signed up to do something, no matter how sick she was feeling, she'd always turn up.'

Laura nodded. 'That's the impression I got of her. Mind you, a good few of my other impressions of her were wrong, so . . .'

'No, she'd never just piss off. Jazzy's a professional.'

'Hm.' Charles made one last attempt. 'Laura, you can't think of anything else, can you? Anything else Jasmine told you about her time in the States . . .?'

'Well, there was one thing. At the stage when our relationship was going really well, when we were even talking of buying a flat together, she did say she'd got about fifteen grand tucked away in a special account. She described it as her "LA haul".'

'Do you think she just meant the money she'd managed to save while she was out there?'

'No, I don't think it was that. From the way she described her life in LA, she was hardly making enough to keep herself clothed and fed, let alone to give her a chance to save any.'

'Well, however she got it,' said Kitty bitterly, 'it's gone now.'

'Really?' Laura looked shocked.

'Last bastard she lived with cleaned her out completely.'

'God, she was always such a bloody idiot when it came to men.'

Charles wanted to get back on to the provenance of the dancer's stash. 'So if Jasmine didn't save it, Laura, where did it come from?'

'Well, I think . . . from things she said . . . that this was some kind of pay-off she'd got from someone.'

'Was she ever more specific about it?'

'She did once describe it as her "hush money".'

'Did she?' said Charles, his mind racing.

FOURTEEN

FIRST BROKER'S MAN: What makes you drink so many
pints of beer?
SECOND BROKER'S MAN: Oh, nothing makes me. I'm a
volunteer.

This time when Charles rang Lefty Rubenstein's mobile there was no answer. So he left the lawyer a message, asking him to return the call. It was frustrating because Charles needed Lefty to validate the chain of logic that was joining up in his head.

Of course there was another line of enquiry Charles had yet to explore, and he felt diffident – not to say a little frightened – to go too far down that route. It was to follow up the information Lefty had given him about the Eastbourne drugs trade.

Still, after a couple of restorative double Bell's, he felt braced for the task. He comforted himself with the thought that he would probably be travelling up a blind alley. The police must have followed the same investigative route, so there was a very strong chance that Eastbourne's dealers would be lying low until the storm blew over.

I don't have much of a genuine detective instinct, Charles mildly chided himself, setting off on a sleuthing mission in the hope I won't find anyone to interview.

The pub whose name Lefty had given him was called the Greyhound, set in the less tourist-friendly part of Eastbourne. There was a broad street called Seaside Road which ran parallel to the front. Though one end joined Terminus Road, Eastbourne's main pedestrian shopping centre, Seaside Road grew shabbier the further east it went. There were more and more ethnic food stores and takeaways, and though there were still some fine Victorian villas, they were not very well maintained and bore the telltale signs of multiple occupancy.

Charles found the Greyhound easily enough. Permanent chalk boards outside promised the usual delights of Sky Sports, Curry Nights, Karaoke and Special Two-for One Meal Deals. Inside, large screens at either end of the bar vied with each other, one providing football, the other music videos. The clientele was not up to that of the Grand Hotel, but it was not as rough as Charles had expected. There was an allowance of shaven-headed men with tattoos and women with hair pulled tightly back from their faces, but there were also respectable-looking pensioners, and even some extended families wading their way through plates piled high with what mostly seemed to be chips.

That sight made Charles feel hungry. He'd only had a sandwich at lunch and that seemed a long time ago. He wondered if eating a meal was a good cover for an undercover operative investigating the drugs trade and decided reluctantly that it wasn't. That decision also affected his choice of drink. If he'd been eating he'd have gone for the red wine. Without food it'd be another large Bell's.

The bar staff didn't look that interested in their clientele, but the one who served him was polite enough. And Charles knew he had to take advantage of that moment of human contact. He had to ask about the name that Lefty had given him. It made him feel rather like the shifty Russian agent he'd played in a television Cold War thriller. ('With Charles Paris representing the Soviet opposition, democracy will be safe for a good few years.' *Observer.*) So, as he took his change, feeling rather embarrassed, he asked, 'Has Vinnie McCree been in tonight?'

To his surprise the girl knew who he was talking about. She looked at her watch. 'He won't be in till later. Always pops in for his couple of pints round nine thirty.'

Charles consulted his watch. Three-quarters of an hour to wait. He would have that meal after all – good idea. He added to his order a rump steak with all the trimmings and a large Merlot.

And then if he lost his bottle before Vinnie McCree arrived, he could at least go back to his digs on a full stomach.

Charles Paris wasn't sure what he expected a drug dealer to look like, but Vinnie McCree certainly wasn't it. A paunchy, balding man in his sixties, he entered the pub wrapped up in an old British

Warm coat. His face was suffused with red, the kind of broken-veined complexion Charles feared he too might have in a few years' time. And Vinnie seemed to be very much a regular – a favourite almost – in the Greyhound. He knew all the bar staff by name and one of them was pulling his pint even before he reached the bar. The girl who had served Charles's large Merlot (and his second one, and the third) had a whispered word with the new arrival and pointed across to where the actor was sitting.

As soon as he'd paid for his pint and taken a large swallow from it, Vinnie came across. 'You were asking for me?' He had quite a thick Scottish accent, but he didn't sound surprised. Maybe Charles's approach was the one used by everyone who wanted to buy drugs.

'Yes,' said Charles, who hadn't really planned this bit of his investigation. All he knew was that the noise from the football analysis and the music videos was too loud for them to worry about being overheard.

'What did you want to see me about?' asked Vinnie.

'A small matter of cocaine.' He didn't feel as airy as he made the words sound.

'Oh, good,' said Vinnie. 'Are you going to sell me some cocaine? Are you a dealer?'

The confusion was quickly sorted out. The two men established that neither of them was actually a drug dealer, and then they had to explain what they were. That Charles Paris was an actor from the cast of *Cinderella* at the Empire Theatre was readily clarified. What Vinnie McCree was doing took a little longer to sort out.

It took so long that the explanation needed to continue past the Greyhound's closing time of eleven o'clock. 'Come back and have another drink at my place,' said Vinnie, and Charles had just reached that level of drunkenness where having another drink anywhere seemed a very good idea. The fact that only half an hour before he'd been prepared to defend himself against an assault from Vinnie McCree now seemed incongruous.

The flat he was taken to was very close – the pub really quali-fied as a 'local' – a shabby conversion in a large shabby house. The hallway smelt of mould and damp, and inside the flat was added a distinct whiff of urine. There was also, Charles realized in the enclosed space, an unwashed sourness emanating from his companion.

Vinnie's home was clumsily designed, with a bathroom separated off by a shoddy partition. There didn't seem to be any evidence of a kitchen area or cooking equipment apart from a kettle. A proliferation of empty bottles suggested that most of the meals Vinnie took were liquid.

And the space was unbelievably untidy, every surface covered, each wall stacked high with newspapers. However much he tried to, Charles couldn't be unaware of the squalor. Nor of comparisons to his own studio flat in Hereford Road in London. Though he hadn't yet reached Vinnie McCree's level of seediness, his own living conditions were moving in that direction. Not for the first time Charles felt that he must take control of his life. Tidy up Hereford Road. Cut down on the drinking.

That thought lasted until Vinnie produced an unopened bottle of Famous Grouse, the whisky that Charles found closest in taste to his beloved Bell's. And once they were both supplied with grubby glasses of the stuff, Vinnie picked up the conversation where they'd left it off. It would have to be described as a conversation, thought Charles, though Vinnie was very definitely doing the lion's share of the talking.

He was, they'd established in the pub, a journalist, but Vinnie didn't seem to think he'd adequately described the kind of journalist he was.

'People who call themselves journalists these days haven't a clue what the job really entails. They sit beside their bloody laptops in Wapping or somewhere, they eat sandwiches and drink bloody mineral water at their desks and they never see the outside world. When I was working in Fleet Street it was very different. Only time we spent in the office was for editorial conferences or sometimes writing up our copy. The rest of the time we were out *finding* bloody stories. Being a journalist back then meant being an investigator. We followed clues, we tracked people down, we made them talk to us – one way or the other we found out the bloody truth!'

'But presumably,' Charles managed to interpolate, 'you're retired now?'

'Well, I don't have a job now, if that's what you mean. Paper had another "rationalization", as they called it, which meant I was out on my ear. Well, you can take away a journalist's job, but you can't take away a journalist's *instinct*. That's what stays with you. That's what stays with *me*. I've still got a nose for a story. If I hear of some injustice, I still want to get to the bottom of it. I've never stopped working. And I'm still capable of getting scoops which the nationals will have to pay me top dollar for. Because they haven't got anyone out there now doing that kind of journalism. Eventually they'll have to fall back on people like me.'

Charles didn't think it was the moment to question how likely that confidence was to be justified. Instead he asked, 'And are you involved in this drugs business because you scent there's a story there?'

'You bet. That's exactly why I'm doing it. And it's going to be a bloody big story. Get a four-page spread in one of the national Sundays – no question about it. "Eastbourne's Drugs Hell" – I can see the headlines now – and the Vincent McCree byline. And it'll be a good story because no one expects that kind of stuff from a nice shooshed-up middle-class town like Eastbourne. No, when they run the story, it's going to be quite an eye-opener for a lot of people. See your glass is empty. Let me top you up.'

While Vinnie made with the bottle of Famous Grouse, Charles said, 'But how did you get involved with Lefty Rubenstein? How come you ended up supplying him with cocaine?'

'Ah.' The journalist looked very pleased with himself. 'Well, this just shows the depth at which I've been working on this story. I've been working on it for a while, getting in with the Eastbourne dealers.'

'At the Greyhound? Is that the place where the trade goes on?'

'Some of it. A few of the guys use the place. But they move around a lot, always keeping one step ahead of the Filth. Have to be clever in their game – and I've had to be just as clever as they are. I pretty soon realized that the only way I was going to find out about how they really worked was to become "embedded" . . . you know, like journalists were during the Iraq War.'

'You mean you had to become part of the drug-dealing operation?'

'Virtually, yes. That's why I thought you might have been a dealer back in the Greyhound, one of my contacts having put you in touch with me. Of course that's the kind of thing I've done a lot through my career. When I started out as a cub reporter on the *Herald* I went undercover to do a feature on Glasgow's gang culture. Nearly got myself killed, of course, but got a damn good story out of it. So what I'm doing here in Eastbourne is kind of going back to my roots.'

'But how far into the drugs network have you penetrated?'

'Oh, I've got a long way in. I'm virtually like a member of the gang now.' Charles was beginning to realize that anything Vinnie McCree said had to be taken with container-loads of salt. 'I started off meeting people down the delivery end, like runners, mostly boys just out of their teens. I bought some stuff off them, just as a way of getting closer to the centre of the organization. And then I decided that the only way I was really going to meet anyone higher up the hierarchy was if I pissed them off. So I bought some cocaine and didn't pay for it.'

'How did you manage that?'

'Easy. I'd arranged to meet the runner down on the sea front. I was in a cab. Soon as the boy had handed over the envelope I told the driver to put his foot down. He didn't get his money. I thought that might cause a bit of a stir. Sure enough, next day a couple of heavies come round here – don't know how they found out my address, but they clearly did, which is a bit worrying. They take me out to their car – I'm not struggling at this point. Once I'm inside they gag me and blindfold me with gaffer tape, shove me down on the floor at the back and drive off somewhere. Then I'm taken into a house – or maybe not a house, a garage or warehouse maybe, and they rough me up a bit.

'Then the gaffer tape's ripped off my eyes and mouth – bloody hurt I can tell you, virtually took my eyebrows off – and I'm face to face with this guy – not one of the heavies, someone else, their boss I imagine – and he tells me what they do to people who steal drugs off them. It was just a warning, but let me tell you – I paid up pretty quick.'

'Did you get a clear look at the boss guy?'

'Not really. His face was in shadow – quite deliberately, I assume. But he did speak with a distinctive accent.'

'Oh?'

'Sort of Eastern European, I think. The heavies didn't say much, but when they did they had similar accents. Romanian, possibly? Albanian? Anyway, my interview with the boss – if that's what he was – was just to put the frighteners on me. The heavies punch me a couple of times in the stomach – hurt a lot, but fortunately that's all they did. Then in no time they've put more gaffer tape over my eyes, I'm hustled out to the car, once again shoved down in the back and they drive me back here, stopping somewhere just round the corner to remove the blindfold. So that's how it happened.'

Charles didn't want to sound picky, but he had to say, 'That doesn't really make it sound as though you're "embedded" in their organization.'

'Ah, but I have a lot of information about them.'

'Not a huge amount. If you can't identify the boss and you still don't know where they took you. Or have you found that out?'

'No,' Vinnie was forced to concede. But then a glint of triumph came into his bleary eyes. 'But I do have something far more important, something that puts me right at the centre of their operations.' He reached into the pocket of his shabby cardigan and produced a mobile phone. 'Never guess where I got this from.'

'No, I'm sure I won't,' said Charles who was wearying a little of Vinnie's self-dramatizing.

'It was just lying in the well of the car at the back, must've slipped out of one of the heavies' pockets. This will be the key, this phone will put me right in there with them.'

'How?'

'Because this phone gets calls giving drug orders.'

'Ah.' Charles could see that that might be potentially relevant to his investigation.

'So,' Vinnie went on, 'I can find out a lot about the organization from the customers, from the people who actually buy the drugs.' He tapped the phone. 'This is my big breakthrough. Finding it was pure luck, but back in my Fleet Street days you always needed a bit of luck. And once things started going my way on a story, then the luck would follow.'

'And have you actually had many calls on the phone, ordering drugs?'

'Only one so far.' The journalist did not allow himself to be cast down for more than a moment, before asserting. 'But I know there'll be others.'

'The one you did have,' asked Charles, 'who was that?'

'We don't deal too much with names in the drugs world,' replied Vinnie, as though he'd spent his whole life as a dealer. 'False names, aliases, maybe. I never did find out the name of the guy who rang last Friday.'

'Did he have an American accent?' asked Charles, warming to the chase.

'Yes, he did. He said he'd been given my number and been told that I could source cocaine for him.'

'So you did?'

'Sure. I'd got plenty of the stuff, which I'd bought from the runners when I started my investigation. So we agreed a price. I asked for quite a lot more than I'd paid for it.'

'Ah, you clearly have a drug dealer's instincts.'

Charles was slightly worried at having said that, but Vinnie took it as a compliment. 'Yes. Anyway, the client didn't seem too worried about how much it cost – his casualness about the price actually made me wish I'd asked for more. But we agreed to meet for the handover.'

'And you say this was Friday night?'

'Yes.'

'Where did you meet?'

'Down by the front.'

'Under the pier?'

'No. In a shelter a little way away from the pier entrance.'

'At street level?'

'Yes. I suggested that for the handover. He was fine about it.'

'So did you talk to him much?'

'Hardly at all. I was already there when he arrived. He asked if I'd got something for him. I counted out the money he gave me.'

'And then handed over the cocaine?'

'No, this guy was just paying for it. He wanted me to deliver it to someone else.' 'What did this guy look like?' Charles asked, simply for confirmation.

'Shortish, round. American accent like I said. Oh, and he had one of those terrible comb-overs.'

There was no question. It had to be Lefty. 'So you've no idea who the guy was?'

'No. We don't deal too much in names in the drug business,' said Vinnie portentously, making himself sound at the same time grandiose and ridiculous.

'Did he stay around?'

'No, he left as soon as he'd told me where to hand over the cocaine.'

'Which was?' asked Charles, knowing the answer.

'He told me there was a guy waiting under the pier. Reddish hair. I just had to hand it over to him. Which I did.' He beamed with self-satisfaction and took a long swallow of Famous Grouse.

'And you didn't recognize the guy?'

'No.'

It was ironic, really. In his fumbling attempts to research the Eastbourne drugs scene, Vinnie McCree had managed to miss what could have been the biggest scoop of his life. If only he'd made the connection and realized that Lefty Rubenstein was sourcing cocaine for Kenny Polizzi, and that he, Vinnie, had actually handed over the drug to the star whose murder was splashed over the front pages of newspapers around the world, then he might have had a story to sell. As it was . . . his failure to recognize the connection seemed emblematic of many other failures in his over-glamourized career.

It was now around two o'clock. The journalist produced another unopened bottle of the Grouse and suggested Charles should stay the night. It was a while, Vinnie said, since he'd had a proper all-night drinking session. 'Of course, it used to happen a lot back in the Fleet Street days. We'd start at El Vino's and then move on, all over the bloody place. Lots of private clubs and . . . Did some of my best work after I'd been drinking all night,' he asserted with tired braggadocio. And, he went on, if Charles did need to kip, there was an old sleeping bag somewhere he could borrow. Go on, it'd be fun to drink all night.

But Charles demurred, saying that he had to be up for rehearsal in the morning. Suddenly the squalor of the flat and the sadness of Vinnie McCree were getting to him. The thought of waking up with a hangover in that noxious place was more than he could contemplate. After fulsome farewells, he left his host and walked the half-mile back to his digs.

Though it had advanced his investigation, meeting Vinnie had shocked him. It had been like looking in a fairground distorting mirror only to realize: No, it was an ordinary mirror. Vinnie McCree was a horrible foreshadowing of what Charles Paris could all too easily become.

FIFTEEN

BARON HARDUP: But what's afoot, I'd like to know?
BUTTONS: Twelve inches, stupid – you're so slow!

Lefty Rubenstein rang at a quarter to eight the following morning. Charles felt infinitely weary, infinitely old and infinitely determined never to drink again.

'You called me.'

'Yes,' said Charles, trying to reassemble his scrambled thoughts. 'It was about Jasmine del Rio.'

'Oh yeah?' Lefty sounded totally uninterested in the information. 'I told you when we met in the hotel, I've never heard the name.'

'I met a friend of hers yesterday . . . well, a former lover actually. Female lover.'

'OK, and . . .?'

'From what the woman said, I think something did happen between Jasmine and Kenny in LA, before he got into *The Dwight House*.'

'It's possible. I don't know everyone he screwed back then. Like I've said before, I wasn't his nursemaid.'

'But I think you did know about this particular hook-up.' Charles knew he was taking a risk. The chain of logic that had seemed so solid the day before now looked tenuous in the extreme. Lefty could destroy it with a couple of words.

But fortunately something Charles had said had brought a note of caution into the lawyer's manner. 'What makes you say that?'

'At the time Jasmine del Rio was going under the name of Marybeth Docker.' Lefty didn't repeat his assertion that he'd never heard the name. He just waited to see what would come next. 'And she was only fourteen years old.' Still no response. 'For some reason someone paid her fifteen thousand pounds – I don't know what that would've been in dollars then – to keep quiet about something. She called it her "hush money".'

'So?' asked Lefty.

'Lilith Greenstone told me you quite often paid hush money to dissuade people from taking legal action against Kenny.'

'Did she? Never liked me, Lilith. Makes a habit of spreading nasty rumours about people . . . particularly Kenny and me. Why are you telling me all this, Charles?'

'Because we said we'd work together on this investigation. If either of us found something out, we'd tell the other.'

'I'm not really sure that you've found anything out, Charles. Just seems to me you're pretty big on conjecture. There's no solid basis to anything you're saying.'

'Well, if there's no solid basis, you won't mind my sharing my conjectures with Detective Inspector Malik, will you?'

'Hey, hey, just a minute. Let's not be hasty here.'

There was a silence. Charles knew he was behaving out of character. Blackmail wasn't a means of persuasion that he liked using. But somehow with Lefty, the arch negotiator, it seemed the right approach. And Charles was finding it easier to do on the telephone than if he had been face to face with the man.

The lawyer picked up the conversation again. 'Let me get this right. You're threatening to take your "conjectures" to Inspector Malik?'

'Yes. What's more, I know where you got the cocaine from too.'

'Well, well, you have been a busy little investigator, haven't you? And am I detecting a veiled threat that you might tell Malik about that too – me supplying Kenny with cocaine?'

'I suppose it's something I could consider, if you don't tell me about the connection between Kenny and Jasmine del Rio.'

'Hm. I'm not sure playing hardball suits you, Charles.'

This observation so closely matched Charles's own feelings that he almost dropped his pretence and owned up, but good sense prevailed and he just said nothing.

'OK,' said Lefty after what felt like a long time. 'I'll even with you, Charles. And one of the reasons that I'll even with you is that I won't be telling you anything I haven't already told Detective Inspector Malik.'

'Really?'

'I had a long session with her yesterday afternoon – well,

afternoon into evening. That's why I didn't reply straight away when I got your message. Malik had already got so much information that there was no point in denying it. I just added a few details for her.'

'Details about Kenny Polizzi and Jasmine del Rio in her Marybeth Docker persona?'

'Yup.'

'And details about you getting cocaine for Kenny?'

'I'm glad to say that subject didn't come up. Malik knew nothing about it . . . well, she knew he'd taken cocaine – the medical examination of the body had revealed that – but she had no idea where it had come from. A state of ignorance, Charles, in which I would like her to remain.'

'OK, I'll keep quiet about that.'

'Thank you.' There was a weary sigh from the other end of the line. 'OK, listen up, Charles. This is what I told Malik. Kenny Polizzi did meet Marybeth Docker when she was out in LA. He never knew that she had another name – nor did he know that she was only fourteen years old. If he'd known that, there was no way he would have screwed her. But he did and . . . well, it was a sensitive time for him out there. They were just doing the final casting rounds for the show that turned out to be *The Dwight House*. Kenny kept getting called back by the producers and then called back again. At that time, had Marybeth Docker gone public – as she threatened to do – that he'd been humping a fourteen-year-old . . . well, it would have been goodbye *Dwight House* – probably goodbye career. So he sent me to negotiate a settlement.'

'The kind of thing that you'd done before?'

'Yes, and the kind of thing I would have to do again, more than once in Kenny's career. Anyway, Marybeth was a tough negotiator.' There was a degree of respect in his voice. 'Eventually we settled on twenty-five thousand dollars. Nearly cleaned Kenny out at the time, because of course the *Dwight House* monies hadn't started coming in yet. But, anyway, that settled it. Marybeth took the money and I believe went back to England with it soon after. Kenny and I never heard anything else from her . . . until suddenly he tells me that she's actually in this *Cinderella* company – except that now she's called Jasmine del Rio.'

'Was he worried when he found that out?'

'He sure was. It made him feel very jumpy. He was worried because he didn't know what she was going to do next.'

'Ask for more money for her continuing silence, I would think.'

'She might have done that, Charles. And that wouldn't have been a problem. We could always have found more money.'

'He was complaining to me that he hadn't got any money.'

'These things are relative. Sure, Kenny was about as good with money as a grizzly bear is with ballroom dancing, but we could always find some. I got accounts in his name he don't even know about. But, anyway, Kenny was afraid it wasn't money this Jasmine was after.'

'What was it, then?'

'He was afraid of her naming and shaming him. Kiss and tell memoir in a Sunday paper. "Kenny Polizzi slept with under-age dancer" – not the kind of headline that'd do a lot for his image. It seems that some of these girls nowadays – I don't know if it's feminism or what, but they seem to take pride in exposing things that should have been forgotten a long time ago. What's that expression they use – "historical sex crimes"?'

'Yes, we've had quite a lot of publicity about that stuff over here recently.'

'In the States too. So Kenny was really scared.'

'And was it an encounter with Jasmine that made him start drinking on the Friday night?'

'First thing was a text from her, wanting to meet and threatening all kinds of nasty publicity if he didn't agree. They did meet, in her car, and she made pretty clear what kind of pay-off she wanted from him. And she fixed that they should meet again later that evening. Under the pier . . . which was kind of a weird place to choose. It was the *prospect* of that second encounter that got him back on the booze.'

'But when we were drinking together early that evening – which must have been after their first meeting – he seemed quite cheerful.'

Lefty didn't see any inconsistency. 'Kenny was a man of volatile moods, particularly when he'd got some vodka inside him.'

'So after you'd got Vinnie McCree to deliver the cocaine to

him, did you hear any more? About how his second meeting with Jasmine had gone?'

'Nothing. Next thing I hear, the guy's dead.'

'So what do you think actually happened when they met?'

'I think she asks him for money – though God knows where she thinks he will have got any from during that evening. They argue, maybe he pulls the gun to scare her, she grabs it and shoots him.'

'Are you sure about that?'

Lefty Rubenstein sighed wearily. 'What else is there to think? I got the impression Detective Inspector Malik's suspicions were moving in that direction too.'

'Did she say so?'

'Not in as many words. But I got the sense that Jasmine del Rio had moved a long way up the suspects' leader board. Look at the facts. There's a text from her on Kenny's phone, fixing the first meeting in her car. Jasmine's most likely the last person to see Kenny alive. Kenny's dead, she's nowhere to be found. I would imagine she's got as far away from Eastbourne as she possibly can. And if that's not an admission of guilt, Charles, I'd like to know what is.'

As Charles made his way to rehearsal, feeling more than ever that he'd spent the night being battered and disoriented in a tumble dryer with a couple of those nubbly plastic balls, his mobile beeped to tell him he'd got a text.

It read: *'If you value your life, don't play Baron Hardup. No one can replace the inimitable Kenny Polizzi.'*

SIXTEEN

DYSPEPSIA: This dress was on offer, a bargain for me.
I got it for a ridiculous figure.
NAUSEA: *So I see!*

C harles was not greatly disturbed by the threat. When
someone has as large a fan base as Kenny Polizzi, there
are bound to be a few cranks out there, some self-
appointed keepers of the flame. For a slightly unhinged devotee,
to regard Baron Hardup being played by someone else as a
personal affront was probably quite logical. What was odd,
though, was that the fan in question had somehow got hold of
Charles's mobile number.

That could suggest a possible link to the *Cinderella* company.
Everyone involved had a copy of the contact sheet prepared by
the stage management, which listed everyone's phone number
and email address.

Charles tried calling the number from which the text had been
sent, but only got a message to say that the phone was switched
off.

Outside the St Asaph's Church Halls, just as he was about to
enter, Charles caught sight of a poster for *Cinderella*. Someone
must have worked hard over the weekend to agree the revised
text and get it printed. All trace of Kenny Polizzi had been
removed from the line-up. Top billing and the largest photograph
now went to Tilly Marcus, 'from TV's *Gatley Road*'. Below her,
in substantially smaller font with a smaller photograph, was Tad
Gentry 'from TV's *Frenton High*'.

Charles anticipated ructions ahead.

Once inside the Church Halls, he immediately got caught up
in rehearsing Baron Hardup and forgot about the threatening text.
In the few moments he had to think about anything other than
Cinderella, the bit of his mind that wasn't full of hangover was
filled by the information he'd received that morning from Lefty.

It seemed that the police suspected Jasmine del Rio of murdering Kenny. But somehow that theory wasn't entirely convincing to Charles.

The absence of two more members of the company was quickly noticed that Tuesday morning. Tad Gentry wasn't there – perhaps sulking about his demotion in the show's billing. But, more disturbing from Charles's point of view, there was no sign of Kitty Woo either. The dancer had been so worried about Jasmine's disappearance that he was concerned that she might have set off on some quixotic quest to find her friend. The company stage manager had tried ringing the missing actors' mobiles and left a series of increasingly urgent messages. But there had been no response from either of them.

Charles wasn't given much chance to worry about Kitty. He found Danny Fitz in a furious state. 'Bix doesn't seem to be aware that we open to the paying public at a two-thirty matinee on Friday. I've had no rehearsal at all for my scenes. Or any of the dialogue scenes, come to that.'

'He's still just working on the choreography, is he?' asked Charles.

'Of course he bloody is. He's still wasting time trying to get those two boneheaded boxers into a dance routine. A totally unnecessary dance routine, I might add. And one that has meant elbowing all of the traditional Broker's Men dialogue. I've been left to rehearse virtually on my own. It was bad enough when we had Mr "International Star" Polizzi shoehorning new bits into the script. I thought the one thing his death would do would be to put a stop to all that, but now everyone in the cast seems to think they have a right to mess up the traditional panto routines.

'And to top it all, bloody Tad Gentry's disappeared. Not that he's any good as an Ugly Sister, but he does occasionally deliver a line he's meant to deliver. And no one can rehearse a double act on their own. Oh, it's so bloody frustrating!'

'Well, look,' Charles suggested, 'would it help if I were to read in Tad's lines for you? Then you can at least get some kind of rehearsal done.'

'Oh, Charles, bless you. Are you sure you wouldn't mind . . .?'

'No problem. Which scene do you want to have a look at?'

'The make-up routine. The one where Nausea and Dyspepsia are getting ready for Prince Charming's ball.'

'OK. What, so we're both sitting behind the dressing table, is that it?'

'Exactly. And when the lights come up we're both holding hand mirrors.'

'Let's go for it, then,' said Charles, finding his place in the script and taking a seat beside Danny. 'So I'll read Nausea.'

'Yes, and you have the first line.'

And so they went into the time-honoured routine . . .

> NAUSEA [HOLDING UP A HAND MIRROR AND LOOKING AT IT]: Aaaargh! Who's that?
>
> DYSPEPSIA [HOLDING UP A HAND MIRROR AND LOOKING AT IT]: Why, that's me.
>
> NAUSEA: Thank goodness. I thought it was me. [LOOKING AGAIN IN THE MIRROR] Actually, you know, I've got the complexion of a sixteen-year-old schoolgirl.
>
> DYSPEPSIA: Well, give it back to her – you're wrinkling it.
>
> NAUSEA: You know, to look really good for Prince Charming's ball, I'm going to have my face lifted.
>
> DYSPEPSIA: When they see what's under it, they'll drop it again pretty damn quick. But, Nausea, you stand no chance with Prince Charming. Not like me. I'm going to appeal to his patriotism. For that reason I've had a pair of knickers made out of a Union Jack.
>
> NAUSEA: Aren't they uncomfortable?
>
> DYSPEPSIA: Well, they were a bit until I took the flagpole out.
>
> NAUSEA: To ensure I really appeal to the Prince I'm going to sprinkle myself all over with toilet water. Have you tried that, Dyspepsia?
>
> DYSPEPSIA: Well, I did once, but the seat fell on my head.
>
> NAUSEA: Oh dear. I've got a new hat for the ball.
>
> DYSPEPSIA: Have you?
>
> NAUSEA: Oh yes. Every time I'm down in the dumps I buy myself a new hat.
>
> DYSPEPSIA: Oh, I wondered where you got them from.

And so it went on. Corny beyond words, but as he watched Danny Fitz working the lines Charles really felt he was seeing a masterclass in comic timing.

And he was flattered when, at the end of the scene, Danny said, 'God, it's such a relief to work with someone who can *act*.'

As if on cue, they were joined from the bigger hall by someone who couldn't act – the real Nausea, Tad Gentry. He was accompanied by Bix Rogers and Tilly Marcus, and the three of them were clearly in the middle of a major row. And the subject of their row Charles found all too predictable.

'Listen, Bix,' Tad was saying, 'if we don't get that poster changed, I'm afraid you're going to have to find someone else to play Nausea. I've just been talking to my agent and she says the contract stipulated that Tilly and I should have *equal* second billing.'

'Yes,' the director argued, 'but now Kenny's dead there is no second billing.'

'Yes, there is – and I've got it. And for some unfathomable reason Tilly's got top billing.'

'The reason is not unfathomable at all,' came the spirited riposte from the lady in question. 'I've got top billing because I'm a regular in *Gatley Road*, which has always had much higher ratings than *Frenton High*.'

'That isn't the point!' stormed Tad.

'I think it's very much the point!' Bix had by now been reduced to the role of spectator, watching the exchange as though he had a seat at the Wimbledon Centre Court. 'Also I am *still* one of the stars of *Gatley Road*, whereas you were dropped from *Frenton High* some years ago.

'I was not *dropped*! I made the decision to leave! I asked the producers to come up with better storylines for my character and when they refused I knew it was the moment to develop my career elsewhere.'

'And where was that exactly?' demanded Tilly. 'I haven't seen much evidence of you being very successful anywhere else. Long time since you've had a part in anything on the box, isn't it?'

'I have been *diversifying* my career,' said Tad with what he hoped was dignity. 'I'd rather outgrown British television. I've been focusing on work in the States.'

'Well, none of it's come to anything, has it? We haven't been treated to any Hollywood blockbusters with you as the star, have we?'

'I did have a part in the new Buck Carty movie.'

'And who the hell's Buck Carty?'

'He's bigger in the States than he is here.'

'He must be.'

'My American agent said it was good to start with a small part . . . you know, it was like a calling card to Hollywood and—'

'Bullshit!' cried Tilly. 'What was the movie called?'

Tad couldn't help looking a little shamefaced as he replied, '*Death of the Undead.*'

'Funny,' said Tilly, enjoying his discomfiture, 'I never heard news of the premiere of that one. Or of the A-list stars who attended it. Straight to video, was it?'

Tad directed his next words to Bix, the ineffectual umpire of the contest. 'This has got to be sorted out,' he said, more calmly. 'My agent says the billing agreement is in the contract. I demand that you get on to the management of this show and have the new poster withdrawn. Otherwise I will be unable to continue in the show.' He looked at his watch. 'You have an hour to sort it out. I'll be in the Starbucks opposite, so come and tell me when we have an agreement.'

And with something approaching dignity, Tad Gentry stalked out of St Asaph's Church Halls.

Without a full complement of Ugly Sisters, there was not a lot for Charles to do, because most of Baron Hardup's scenes involved Nausea and Dyspepsia. Anyway, after Tad's departure Danny had also stormed out in a fit of pique, so they were left with no Ugly Sisters.

The one other scene he could have rehearsed was near the beginning of the show, when the Broker's Men came and demanded Baron Hardup's overdue rent. But since Mick 'The Cobra' Mesquito and Garry 'Bomber' Brawn were still involved with Bix trying to translate boxing into dance, they couldn't do that one either.

Charles checked with the stage management that he wasn't required for anything else and, having assured them he'd have his mobile switched on in case of a sudden call, left the hall.

He'd decided, for the second time in two days, that he might go to a coffee shop.

*   *   *

Charles Paris wasn't very well informed about the infinite varieties of coffee available in a Starbucks, but he did know that he liked a double espresso, so that was what he ordered.

While it was being prepared he looked across at Tad, who sat without newspaper or book, staring down into his coffee cup. Though not familiar with *Frenton High*, a series about the loves, feuds and other extramural disasters of a group of surprisingly attractive (and surprisingly old-looking) sixth-formers at a London comprehensive school, Charles had gathered that Tad's character had been a fatally attractive villain. And the much-disputed photograph on the *Cinderella* poster dated from the height of his soap-star fame. In it he was strikingly good-looking, with his black hair and almost black eyes.

But the Tad Gentry who sat in Starbucks that Tuesday morning was no longer quite such a babe magnet. Though his body was still meticulously gym-toned, his face had thickened out a bit around the jowls. His hair, even blacker now, so much so that it must have been dyed, was beginning to thin around the temples. And the lips that might once have been sensuous now just looked petulant.

Though they had spent no time in a one-to-one situation, the two actors did obviously know each other as members of the *Cinderella* company, so it was quite legitimate for Charles to move across with his espresso and say, 'Mind if I join you?'

Tad shrugged permission without notable enthusiasm. Charles decided that he should ingratiate himself a little. 'Sorry to hear about that business in the rehearsal room. They are buggers, aren't they? Never seem to take any notice of what's in your contract.'

'Tell me about it,' said Tad.

'And it's ridiculous giving Tilly billing above you.'

Charles worried for a moment that he was taking self-ingratiation too far, but the younger actor's response showed he'd got the approach just right.

'Yes, I mean the fact is that Matt Luckworth was a kind of iconic figure.' Charles hoped he was right in assuming that this was the name of the character Tad had played in *Frenton High*. To have to ask about it might show a lack of respect for the triumphant high spot of the young actor's career.

His conjecture was quickly confirmed. 'I mean, people still talk about him as sort of *the* villain. One of the great villains. Like Macbeth or Moriarty or Hannibal Lecter.'

Charles thought Tad was possibly pitching his comparisons a bit high, but he made no comment on that, instead saying, 'You must have been really gutted when they decided to write the character out.'

'They didn't write the character out,' Tad insisted. 'It was my choice to leave. Didn't you hear what I was saying to that cow Tilly? I asked the producers for stronger Matt Luckworth storylines or I'd go. They said they couldn't guarantee me stronger storylines, so I called their bluff and went. It was the producers who were gutted then. What they must've thought when they saw the media coverage Matt's death in the motorbike accident got. The *Sun*'s headline was "TV's Smouldering Mr Sex Goes Up In Smoke". One of the tabloids even said they thought *Frenton High* wouldn't survive without my character in it. Because my profile was really high. I was getting lots of offers then.'

'What – the RSC? The National?'

Tad shook his head testily. 'No, much higher profile stuff than that. They were going to have me on *I'm A Celebrity, Get Me Out Of Here*, but it turned out that they'd already booked a male soap star. Then there was a suggestion that I might present the Midweek National Lottery. And talks went quite a long way on having me on *Strictly Come Dancing*.'

Clearly there was quite a gap between Charles Paris's views of career fulfilment and those of Tad Gentry.

'But I couldn't commit myself for that length of time, you know, with things that were happening in the States.'

'What things actually were happening in the States?' asked Charles respectfully.

'Well, I'd got my American agent set up in LA and I went over for a few months, because he said casting interviews tended to be set up at very short notice in Hollywood.'

'Yes, I'm sure they are.'

'And, you know, it was useful networking time for me. He fixed invitations for me at movie premieres, that kind of thing. It's getting your face seen in the right places that matters out there, you know.'

'So I've heard. And of course you got to work with Buck Carty,' said Charles, congratulating himself on remembering the name he'd never heard before that morning.

'Oh yes.'

Pushing his self-ingratiation to the edge of sycophancy, Charles then asked the ultimate amateur question, the one put to anyone who's been even on the furthest fringes of celebrity. 'What's Buck really like?'

Tad coloured. 'Well, I didn't actually have any scenes with him. My character was more involved in the subplot, really.'

'Ah. Right.'

There was a kind of method in Charles's approach to Tad. He was shamelessly bolstering the young man's self-esteem for a reason. Which came out in his next question. 'Did you actually meet Kenny Polizzi while you were out in LA?'

For the first time a look of caution came into the black eyes. 'Why do you ask that?'

'I just remember his first day of rehearsal, last Wednesday, you greeted him like you knew him.'

'Yes.' Tad was embarrassed by the recollection. 'Well, we had met at a party given by Julia Roberts.' Charles noticed how the occasion had been upgraded from 'the premiere of that Julia Roberts movie'. 'Kenny and I had quite a long chat about the entertainment scene in the UK. He'd had some offers to do stuff over here, and he was asking my advice on what was worth doing.' That such a conversation had ever taken place sounded deeply unlikely to Charles, but he said nothing as Tad went on, 'But now of course over here Kenny Polizzi was the big star, wasn't he? He was embarrassed to admit he'd asked career advice from anybody, particularly someone who wasn't Hollywood. That's why he froze me out, pretended he'd never seen me before.'

Charles was flabbergasted by these obvious lies, but still made no comment. Tad had clearly got himself to the point of actually believing them. 'I can see,' he said, 'why you're angry about Tilly Marcus getting bigger billing than you are, but how did you feel when you saw the size of Kenny's billing on the original poster?'

'Well, I was a bit pissed off, I have to confess. I mean, I know Kenny's supposed to be an international star and all that, but *The*

Dwight House finished years ago. And if you go along with Tilly's view that I should get lower billing because I'm no longer in *Frenton High*, well, the same thing goes for Kenny, but even more so.'

'Yes, but I suppose *The Dwight House* is something of an international television phenomenon.'

'*Frenton High* sells abroad too. It's very popular in Kazakhstan.'

'Is it?' Charles moved off on another tangent. 'Apparently there's still no sign of Jasmine del Rio.'

Tad shrugged. The news was of no interest to him.

'It's odd, though, isn't it?'

'I don't really see why. So some tart of a dancer breaks her contract. So what?'

'You didn't have anything to do with her . . . you know, on a personal level?'

'God, no. I mean, obviously she fancied me, but over the years I've got used to that. And once last week when we were having a drink together, she made it pretty clear that if I wanted to shag her, I had only to say the word.' He allowed himself a thin smile. 'An offer that I didn't take up. I do have my standards.'

'So you wouldn't have any idea where Jasmine might have disappeared to?'

'Absolutely none.' Tad looked up at the approach of a rather agitated young female stage manager from the *Cinderella* company. 'Ah,' he said, 'news at last of the management's climb-down.' He grinned at Charles. 'Never fails, calling people's bluff.'

'Tad,' said the stage manager. 'I've got a message from Bix.'

'Oh, great.' The actor picked up the designer leather bag he'd left on the seat beside him. 'I'll come back straight away, then.'

'No.' The stage manager, now looking very nervous indeed, raised a hand to stop him. 'Bix says he's been on to the producers. They say it's far too late to change the show's billing, even if they wanted to. But they don't want to. They accept your resignation from the *Cinderella* company.'

'What!'

'They'll be on to your agent to sort out the contractual details.' The stage manager's delivery speeded up as she neared the end of her unwelcome task (which shouldn't have been delegated to her but been done face-to-face by Bix Rogers). 'If you've got

any belongings left in the rehearsal room, then you're requested
to pick them up straight away.'

'I don't have anything . . .' he gestured rather ineffectually to
his bag '. . . except this.'

'That's fine, then. Goodbye.' And the stage manager scuttled
out of Starbucks like a terrified kitten.

'Well, isn't that just bloody typical!' said the former soap star.
'That Tilly Marcus is behind it. She's been twisting Bix's arm,
I know. She's been worried about me from the start. Scared of
being shown up in a production with someone so much more
talented than she is in it.'

It seemed appropriate for Charles to say, 'I'm sorry.'

'Oh, don't worry. Doing this show was always going to be a
bit of a bind, tying me down here in Eastbourne when I should
be following up opportunities in London and the States.'

Charles thought it would be churlish to mention how few
opportunities for actors there would be in London during the
weeks running up to Christmas.

He also got the strong impression that Tad Gentry wasn't very
good at choosing his moments to call people's bluffs.

SEVENTEEN

DYSPEPSIA: You know, a man once said to me
I looked like one of those teenage ravers.
NAUSEA: Well, whoever that man might be,
He should have gone to Specsavers!

TV's Mr Sex stormed out of Starbucks rather petulantly. Tad said he'd check the contractual situation with his agent, and then probably explore flights to LA. He'd thought for some time that the main focus of his career from now on should be in the States. A lot of young British actors were doing really well out there.

As Charles walked back to the St Asaph's Church Halls, the number of dancers smoking outside it told him that they'd reached the lunch break. And he was pleased to see that amongst them was Kitty Woo, alone, arms clasped around herself against the cold, sucking sustenance from a cigarette.

'Hi. Are you all right? I was worried you weren't at rehearsal.'

'I'm OK, Charles. Well, a bit battered, but I'll survive.'

'Battered? You mean someone's beaten you up?'

'No. Emotionally battered. I've just had another long session with Detective Inspector Malik.'

'Oh, really? About Jasmine?'

'You bet. They seem, like, extremely keen to find her.'

Charles was unsurprised by the news. From what Lefty Rubenstein had said, it sounded like Jasmine del Rio was the police's primary suspect for the role of murderer.

'I've just been having a coffee with Tad. You heard he was out of the show, did you, Kitty?'

'No, I only just got back here when they were breaking for lunch. What's all this about, then?'

Charles gave a brief résumé of the morning's events, from Tad's spat with Tilly Marcus to his confrontation with the stage manager in Starbucks. Kitty grinned wryly. 'Can't say he's any great loss. Have you heard who they're getting in to replace him?'

'No, I've only just come back from the coffee shop. No doubt it'll be another boxer,' Charles suggested mischievously.

'I wouldn't put it past them.' Kitty took a ferocious pull on her cigarette. She looked very wretched.

'Did you get any impression from Detective Inspector Malik whether the police are suspicious of Jasmine?'

'You mean putting her in the frame as the murderer?'

'Yes, all right. That's what I did mean.'

'Hm . . .' Kitty wrinkled her nose. 'Don't know. Malik just said that finding Jazzy was their number-one priority. I suppose that could mean they've got her down as the murderer. But I kinda got the impression . . .' A sob shuddered through her slender frame, cutting off her words.

'What impression, Kitty?'

'The impression that Malik thought something might have happened to Jazzy.'

'By "something happened" do you mean she might be dead?'

'I sort of got the feeling that's what Malik was hinting at.'

'Did she have any reason for suggesting that?'

'If she did she wasn't about to share it with me.'

'No surprise there. Did you get any suggestion from Malik that she knew about the connection between Jasmine and Kenny Polizzi?'

'Oh yes, she knew all about that.'

'How? You didn't tell her, did you?'

'No. Laura Hahn did.'

'Really? Why would she do that?'

'She's so worried about Jazzy's disappearance. Laura reckoned telling everything she knew to the police might help them find her.'

'Hm . . .' Charles was silent for a moment. Then he said, 'I was thinking about something you said at lunchtime on Sunday . . .'

'Oh yeah?'

'We were talking about whether anyone in the *Cinderella* cast had come on to Jasmine . . .'

'I remember.'

'And you sort of implied that someone might have come on to her and she might have gone out and had a drink with him.'

'Mm.'

'Did that actually happen?'

'Yes, it was like, first, second day of rehearsals. She came to the digs after she'd been with him and we had a right old giggle.'

'What was so funny about it?

'Well, he'd come on to her all smooth and chatty and after they'd had a drink he asked Jazzy back to his digs and she's, you know, a game girl and she hadn't had any action for quite a while, so she was a bit randy and . . . Anyway . . .' Kitty Woo let out a throaty giggle '. . . when they actually got into bed, in spite of his smooth talk and all that, he couldn't get it up!'

This prompted another wave of hilarity. Charles waited till it had subsided, then said, 'You've very deliberately avoided telling me the name of the man in question.'

'Yes, I have, haven't I?' Another short burst of giggles. 'It was Tad Gentry.'

'Ah,' said Charles. 'Was it?'

And he wondered how 'TV's Mr Sex' would feel towards a woman who had witnessed him failing to get an erection.

Charles wasn't reckoning on a lot of rehearsal for him that afternoon. Even though the first public performance of *Cinderella* was a mere three days away, almost all of Baron Hardup's scenes were with the Ugly Sisters, and the production was currently one short in the Ugly Sister department.

Or so he'd assumed. But when he arrived back in the smaller rehearsal room he was surprised to see on Danny Fitz's face the biggest smile – and indeed the only smile – he had ever witnessed.

'What's happened?' Charles asked.

'Finally something good.' There was also more animation in Danny's manner that he had ever witnessed. 'The first sensible decision that has been made throughout this entire benighted production.'

'Tell me more.'

'Well, the first bit of undiluted good news is that that charm-free, talent-free bonehead Tad Gentry is no longer in the show.'

'Yes, I did know about that.'

'But the even better news is that Bix has finally listened to one of my ideas.'

'Oh?'

'For the replacement, for the actor to play Nausea.'

'So who is it?'

'I wonder if you're too young, Charles, to have heard of Arthur Bodimeade.'

'Certainly not. He was a legend in the theatre. But surely he can't still be around, can he?'

'He's very much around. He's ninety-four years old and he lives right here in Eastbourne. What's more, Bix agreed to let me offer him the part of Nausea and – the even better news – Arthur's agreed to step into the breach.'

As if on a cue, the rehearsal-room door opened to admit a little old man, whose overcoat must've fitted when he had more flesh on his bones. Now he looked like a stick insect wrapped in a towel. The skin on his face was parchment-thin and he wore round glasses with lenses as thick as the bottoms of jam jars. What hair remained on his head had been dyed jet black and Brylcreemed down as though there was still enough of it to have a parting. One freckled, claw-like hand carried a dark grey trilby, the other a small leather suitcase. His black shoes had a high polish rarely seen outside military establishments.

Arthur Bodimeade and Danny Fitz were clearly old friends. And there was a wonderful physical contrast between them, Danny built like a docker, Arthur tiny and bird-like. When introduced to Charles Paris the newcomer said, 'Yes, of course, I have heard your name, but probably not seen much of your recent work. I don't find it so easy to get to the theatre these days.'

'Well, it's a real honour to meet you. I've heard so much about you.'

Arthur Bodimeade's watery eyes twinkled. 'Nothing too bad I hope.'

'All good.'

'Flatterer,' came the almost skittish response.

'And I am delighted to see that you are still working,' said Charles.

'Oh, I do still get offers,' said Arthur Bodimeade. 'The trouble is these days they all seem to be for old men.'

EIGHTEEN

FAIRY GODMOTHER: My magic powers and inspiration
Now will make . . . a transformation!

Charles Paris found that afternoon's rehearsal a wonderful education. If watching Danny Fitz work on his own had been a masterclass, then some more elevated description would have to be found for the interplay between Danny and Arthur Bodimeade. They referred to various traditional panto-mime routines in a kind of shorthand. 'Can we fit in the Drink of Truth here, do you think?' 'Let's do the Money Lending Gag.' 'Is this the moment for the Busy Bee?'

And each, by some kind of instinct, knew exactly what followed. Though the two actors had never actually worked together, they came from the same tradition. The physical contrast between them made for a perfect double act. And they were walking repositories of pantomime history.

The other remarkable sight Charles observed that afternoon was the transformation of Arthur Bodimeade. Frail and doddery when he wasn't acting, the moment he started the crosstalk with Danny Fitz, the years dropped off him. He was suddenly light on his feet, lithe as a teenager. Actors describe the magic that enables someone laid up with crippling flu to go on stage and give a fine performance as 'Doctor Theatre'. And Doctor Theatre was certainly doing his stuff with Arthur in that rehearsal room.

The most astonishing achievement of the afternoon was the emergence of a script. The scenes Danny had been trying to get together with Tad had had no life and felt like clumsy irrelevances bolted on to the *Cinderella* story. But the routines he worked up with Arthur had their own kind of logic and pushed the narrative forward. The two old actors were clearly adept at tailoring their material to different storylines. With slight adjustments their routines could be – and had been – fitted in to any pantomime from *Aladdin* to *Babes in the Wood*. With minor word changes and the interpolation of a few characters' names, the script they ended up with that afternoon could have been written specifically for *Cinderella*.

Baron Hardup's contributions to the Ugly Sisters' scenes had never amounted to a great deal, just the odd feed line to throw in, and with the new routines he had even less to do, but Charles couldn't have minded less. Like most actors (though they all deny it) the first thing he did on receiving a new script was to count his lines, and like most actors he felt pretty miffed when one or more of them was cut. But working with Danny Fitz and Arthur Bodimeade was such a treat that he wouldn't have cared if he had no lines at all in their scenes. He was getting enough of a charge from being in the presence of genius.

At the end of the afternoon's rehearsal, Charles suggested that he should treat Danny and Arthur to a drink at the Sea Dog, but both demurred. Danny said he wasn't really a pub person, and Arthur said he was too tired. And indeed, out of the panto routines, he did look every one of his ninety-four years. Charles wondered how that frail frame would stand up to the challenge of two shows a day, matinee and evening, from Monday to Saturday for the six-week run. He hoped Doctor Theatre would be able to keep up the good work.

So Charles was sitting alone in the Sea Dog with a post-rehearsal large Bell's. The wonders of the afternoon had driven thoughts of Kenny Polizzi and Jasmine del Rio out of his head, but now they came crashing back in.

He was particularly intrigued by Kitty's news that Detective Inspector Malik and her team seemed to be pointing at Jasmine as Kenny's murderer, and tried to work out why that might be the case. Of course he didn't know how much the police knew. It was quite possible – indeed almost certain – that they had evidence of which he knew nothing.

But the scenario that was taking shape in his head, that Jasmine had wanted to blackmail Kenny, didn't give her any motive to kill him. In fact, she'd very definitely have wanted to keep him alive, a ready and continuing supply of hush money. Her secret had become more valuable with the passage of years. A minor actor in Hollywood going to bed with a fourteen-year-old girl wasn't big news. But the star of *The Dwight House* having gone to bed with a fourteen-year-old girl . . . that was very different, particularly in these days when there was a voguish obsession with 'historical' sex crimes.

The other possibility, that Jasmine had been so traumatized by her under-age sexual experience with Kenny that she had nursed a hatred of him for years until she finally got the chance to expiate it by killing him, just didn't work for Charles. From what he'd seen of Jasmine – and from what Kitty had said about her friend – she was a pretty tough cookie. And with a precocious sexuality. It was even possible, given her character, that she might have been the instigator of the sexual encounter.

In Charles's mind, the one thing that might suggest some guilt attached to Jasmine del Rio was her disappearance. The timing, the fact that she hadn't been seen since Kenny's murder, did perhaps justify some suspicion.

But Charles definitely agreed with Detective Inspector Malik that the next step to solving the crime must involve finding Jasmine del Rio.

Charles wasn't very good at checking his mobile phone for messages. It didn't really ring that often. And he was even worse at checking it for text messages. He had switched off the alert tones so as not to disturb rehearsals, which was a good thing. Mobile phones going off were very unpopular with directors. But he kept forgetting to switch the alerts back on again.

Now in the Sea Dog, having just been up to the bar for his second large Bell's (and having left his *Times* crossword in his digs), he decided to check his text messages.

There was only one. It read: *'Don't try stepping into Kenny Polizzi's shoes. Or you'll end up the same way he did.'*

Again Charles tried calling the number from which the text had been sent. Again there was no response.

Foolishly he'd deleted the former threatening text, so he couldn't check whether they were sent from the same phone. The number didn't look familiar, though.

This new threat shook him up a bit, certainly more than the first one had done. It was effectively saying that if he continued to play Baron Hardup, he would be killed. And after what had happened to Kenny he knew there was someone out there ready to put that threat into action.

He wondered what he should do, what action he should take. He supposed the obvious course would be to tell Detective Inspector Malik. The texts might be significant to her enquiries. But something in him was reluctant to take that step. Was it possibly because of his agreement to share information with Lefty Rubenstein, as though the two of them were conducting their own investigation?

Even as he had the thought, his mobile rang. The call was from Lefty – more synchronicity perhaps?

'So what's new?' asked the lawyer.

'Well, I've discovered that last week Jasmine del Rio had a minor fling with another cast member.'

'Minor? What does that mean?'

Charles told Lefty exactly why the skirmish with Tad Gentry qualified as 'minor'. He concluded, 'If it turns out that something's happened to Jasmine, then that could bring Tad into the frame as a suspect. She'd really put his nose out of joint.'

'Sounds like it wasn't just his nose. You got anything else, Charles?'

'Nothing major. What about you?'

'Well, I've just come back from another interview with Detective Inspector Malik. One very persistent lady she is.'

'Yes. Did you get anything new from her?'

'Not really. But she did ask me not to go back to the States for a few days.'

'What, she's forbidden you to travel?'

'It wasn't put quite like that. She behaved with characteristic British decorum. It would be "more convenient for her enquiries" if I were to remain here in England. Just for a little while until the direction of her investigation became clearer.'

'And did she imply it was becoming clearer?'

'She sounded very confident, but I don't know what that confidence was based on.'

'And she's still no nearer tracking down Jasmine?'

'It seems not, no.'

There was a silence, then Charles asked: 'You haven't been getting any anonymous text messages, have you?'

'No. Why? Have you?'

'I've had a couple.'

'What have they been saying?'

Charles told Lefty about the two texts he'd received. 'But I haven't a clue where they might have come from.'

'Hm. Well, given what they say, I just might have an idea on that.'

'Really?'

'Does the name Gloria van der Groot mean anything to you?'

'Yes, I met her with Kenny after rehearsal one night. His Number One Fan?'

'Exactly. Well, I figure she'd be the Number One Suspect for having sent those texts to you. In her mind no one can replace Kenny in any capacity. I guess she feels your taking over his part is showing disrespect to his memory.'

'Oh, great. But is she dangerous? I mean, is she likely to carry out her threats?'

'I'd be very surprised if she did. I've never actually met her – the Lord be praised – but from what Kenny said, she's just a weirdo. I think most of what happens in her life happens inside her head.'

'I'm not sure that's the most reassuring answer I've ever heard, Lefty.'

'Don't worry about it, Charles. You'll be safe. For one thing, I think Gloria has already gone back to the States.'

'Oh well, that is a relief, thanks. You say you haven't had any anonymous texts. Have you had any from Gloria in the last few days, I mean, since Friday?'

'Yeah. Kenny would never let her know his cellphone number, but, typically, he made sure she'd got mine. It got to the point years ago where if I saw a text was from her I'd delete it. But Kenny made me stop that. He said he needed to know what she was up to.'

'And did she stalk him?'

'Kind of. But she never did anything actionable. She just somehow always managed to find out where he was going to be, and she'd be there too. She'd never try to gain entrance to any of his houses or the hotel rooms where he was staying. She was just like a fixture in his life.'

'And you say you've recently had a text from her?'

'I've had a couple.'

'Saying what?'

'Following on really from what she's sent to you. She thinks that for the management to continue with the production of *Cinderella* after what happened to Kenny is sacrilege. She somehow thinks I have the power – or the inclination – to get them to pull the plug on the show.'

'Hm.' There was a silence between them. Charles heard raucous laughter from a corner of the Sea Dog bar. 'Incidentally, Lefty, do you know if the police have spoken to Gloria van der Groot?'

'Why should they have? I doubt they know she exists. I certainly haven't mentioned her to them. Have you?'

'No.'

'Why do you ask?'

'Well, I was just thinking . . . The woman's pretty close to being a stalker. She always used to hang around wherever Kenny was. Did she ever follow him in the street, that kind of thing?'

'Yes. I kept discouraging her, texting her to say how much Kenny valued his privacy, but it didn't stop her.'

'Well, if that was the case . . .'

'Yes?'

'There's a possibility she might have stalked him on Friday night, that she might actually have seen what did happen to him.'

'Unlikely, but I suppose it's just possible.'

'You must have her cellphone number.'

'Yeah, but like I say she's gone back to the States.'

'I'd still be interested to talk to her.'

'OK' Lefty didn't sound keen on the idea, but he did give Charles the number. As soon he and Lefty had finished their call, he tried ringing it. No response. No invitation to leave a message.

Charles Paris felt frustrated. He also felt hungry. He ordered the Sea Dog's sausage and mash, reflecting that the last time he'd eaten that particular dish he'd been in the exotic company of Lilith Greenstone. Oh well . . . Particularly nice Gloucester Old Spot sausages. And he ordered a large Merlot to wash it down.

While he ate, he had his mobile on the table next to his plate. Otherwise he might not have noticed the arrival of a text message.

All it said was: '*Jasmine del Rio?* Ranleigh Road.'

*   *   *

It seemed reasonable – or at least a good starting point – to assume that the road was in Eastbourne. The girl behind the bar at the Sea Dog helpfully produced a local map for Charles to find out how to get there. It was some way from the sea, more in the direction of the Greyhound pub than the town's main tourist attractions.

As he walked through the moonlit night, Charles wondered what he would do when he reached his destination. He had only a street name, after all. Would he bang on every front door and asked if anyone had seen Jasmine del Rio? He somehow doubted that that would be a very fruitful approach.

But when he reached the road specified, he realized his problem was going to be a rather different one. There were no houses. He found himself in a kind of service road, lined on one side by the back yards and loading bays of a row of shops. The walls, fences and gates were graffiti-scored and in most cases razor-wire-topped. On the other side of the road was a row of run-down garages or lock-ups.

Well, at least the situation restricted Charles's options. Since there were no front doors to bang on, he would begin by focusing his attention on the row of lock-ups. There was fortunately sufficient light for him to see what he was doing, but he didn't approach the task with much optimism. Most of the garage doors seemed to have been locked for millennia. Some had built up an accretion of rusty rings and hooks and hasps and padlocks. Some hung a little drunkenly from their hinges, suggesting that, even if they could be unlocked, tugging them open would still present a major difficulty.

Charles went along the row, seeing if there were any signs that one had been recently opened. But it had rained heavily the last two nights and any clues there might have been had been washed away into the metal-covered gutter which ran along parallel to the locked doors.

As he passed lock-up after lock-up, Charles tried the handles of the doors to see if any might give a little. He'd nearly finished the row when he came to one which had a metal up-and-over door with a T-shaped handle in the middle.

Thinking that he would soon be back in his digs with that comforting bottle of Bell's, he turned the handle and made a lifting movement.

To his amazement the door responded. Making a rattling, scraping sound, very loud in the night-time, the door swung up above his head and slid back into the ceiling of the garage.

Parked in the space revealed was a car that looked almost like a full-size toy. Charles Paris had never seen one before, but it was a Mint Green Nissan Figaro.

He wished he'd brought a torch. Though the moon was nearly full its light didn't penetrate into the shadows of the lock-up. He moved gently forward on the driver's side of the Figaro and felt his way along till he found the door handle. Not daring to hope it might be unlocked, he gave it a sharp tug.

He was aware of an unpleasant smell, as the overhead light inside the car came on. It revealed Jasmine del Rio slumped back in the driver's seat. Just like Kenny Polizzi, she had a neat bullet hole in the centre of her forehead.

NINETEEN

*FIRST BROKER'S MAN: The police are looking for a man
with one eye, it's true.*
*SECOND BROKER'S MAN: Oh, they're so lazy. You'd think
they'd look with two.*

N ow he knew he was at a crime scene, Charles regretted
having left his fingerprints on the door handle. A
cautious part of him said that he should touch nothing
else and immediately ring the police. A more curious, less law-
abiding part of him said he should quickly check a couple of
details and then ring the police.

There was surprisingly little blood, though Charles noticed
that what there was had spattered onto the headrests of both
seats. In Jasmine del Rio's right hand, which lay on her lap, was
a pistol. Charles didn't know a lot about guns, but he reckoned
it looked very similar to the one that he had seen Lefty give
Kenny outside the Sea Dog.

The dead girl's left hand had dropped palm up onto the
passenger seat. Looking as if it had slipped from her grasp lay
an iPhone. Charles moved round to the other side of the Figaro.
Now remembering to cover his hand with a handkerchief, he
opened the passenger-side door and picked up the mobile. He
leant into the car to take advantage of the overhead light.

Charles wasn't familiar with the wonders of the iPhone. All
he required of his own mobile was that it allowed him to make
and receive calls and texts, but he did remember Kitty saying
something about her friend always 'scribbling down stuff on the
little Notes app'. Needless to say, he had no idea what a 'little
Notes app' was, but once he'd managed to switch the phone on,
he was presented with a screen of unfamiliar coloured icons. One
of these had a yellow strip at the top of a row of lines, and
underneath was the word 'Notes'.

With a handkerchief-covered finger he pressed it, and was

immediately rewarded with what was presumably the last note Jasmine del Rio had ever written.

It read: '*I thought killing Kenny would also kill the pain I have suffered all these years. In fact it's made it worse. I can't go on. Sorry.*'

'It seems to be becoming something of a habit for you, Mr Paris,' said Detective Inspector Malik. 'Finding murder victims.'

Charles found himself unexpectedly nervous and gabbled a response. 'And I suppose if a person who finds one body automatically makes themselves suspicious, someone who discovers two makes themselves even more suspicious.' He thought it was a sentence that Oscar Wilde would have phrased better.

'Yes,' said Malik. And there was no irony in her black eyes.

Charles Paris was asked if he would mind going down to the station for some questioning, and it wasn't put in a way that made 'No' a viable response.

Once there he was asked if he minded his mobile being taken away for experts to see if they could trace the source of the anonymous texts. Then he found himself sitting at a table opposite Detective Inspector Malik. There was also a male uniformed policeman sitting in the corner. Charles was once again asked if he minded having their conversation recorded. He said he didn't mind.

'Obviously,' Malik began, 'what interests us is how you came to find Jasmine del Rio's body.'

Her manner was a little different from the last time she had interviewed him. She seemed more relaxed, less urgent, as though perhaps she had reached, or was on the verge of, some breakthrough on the case.

'I told you, Inspector. I had a text message.'

'And you say you have no idea who it was from.'

'Well, it's the third anonymous text I've had since Kenny Polizzi's death and they all came from different numbers.'

'That's no surprise. In the criminal world there are quite a lot of mobiles that are only used once and then thrown away.'

'I thought they could be traced.'

'It depends how effectively they've been thrown away. If you're operating in Eastbourne there's a whole lot of sea out there.'

'Of course.'

'And you say the first two texts were warning you off taking over Kenny Polizzi's role in the pantomime?'

'Yes.'

'So surely you must have some idea who might not want you playing Baron Hardup?'

'Well, I was talking recently to Lefty Rubenstein, who's Kenny Polizzi's—'

'I know who Mr Rubenstein is, Mr Paris. I have spoken to him extensively.'

'Of course you would have done. Well, did he at any point mention to you a woman called Gloria van der Groot?'

'No, he didn't.'

So Charles quickly brought the Inspector up to speed with what he knew of Kenny Polizzi's Number One Fan.

'A stalker?'

'Yes. So far as I can tell, a fairly harmless one. I mean, I did once meet her with Kenny. He was polite to her. I think she represented a nuisance rather than a threat.'

Detective Inspector Malik made a note on her iPad. 'We'd better talk to her.'

'I think that might be difficult. According to Lefty Rubenstein, she's gone back to the States.'

'I'm sure we can track her down. Do you know where she was staying in Eastbourne? Which hotel?'

'It was a B&B.'

Malik grimaced. 'We've got a good few of those here.'

'Yes, sorry I can't be more helpful. Don't know any more details.'

'We can check. And check flight records to see when she left the country.'

At that moment they were interrupted by a knock on the door and the entrance of a uniformed policeman with Charles's mobile.

'We've checked the numbers the texts came from, Inspector. No trace of any of them.'

'As I thought. Thank you.' Detective Inspector Malik dismissed the policeman. 'Going back to Gloria van der Groot, Mr Paris . . .'

'Yes. I did have a thought about her . . .'

'Oh?'

'Well, that if she had a habit of stalking, following Kenny Polizzi, she might have been doing that on the night he died.'

'And therefore be a very valuable witness? Good idea, Mr Paris.' More notes on the iPad. 'Don't worry, we'll track her down. It'd be good to fill in a few gaps in Friday night's sequence of events.'

'Is it sort of coming together?'

It was a question he wouldn't have dared to ask to the sterner Detective Inspector Malik of his previous encounter, and she was surprisingly forthcoming in her reply. 'We've pieced together a lot of details. I don't know if you know that Mr Polizzi was actually under the pier to buy some cocaine.'

'Oh really?' said Charles, a little confused. He obviously did know that, but he couldn't remember whether the Inspector knew he knew. Once again he was unwilling to land Lefty Rubenstein in the soup.

'Well, we've found the man he got the cocaine from. We visited him at his home this afternoon. He gave us some cock-and-bull story about being a journalist investigating Eastbourne's drug trade, but he's clearly just a rather incompetent dealer. He'll be prosecuted once we've tied up this case. But he was very useful – he gave us a description of what went on under the pier for at least part of the evening.'

Interesting, thought Charles. Perhaps Vinnie McCree saw more than he'd let on during their Monday night conversation. Perhaps he stayed around the pier area for longer than he had implied. An official police interrogation might have jogged his memory, particularly if he was under threat of prosecution. Charles made a mental note to have another chat with Vinnie McCree.

'If we can find this . . .' Malik went on, consulting her iPad, '. . . Gloria van der Groot then we'll begin to see the whole picture. And I guess we really have to thank you, Mr Paris.'

'Oh?' Charles was puzzled. 'What for?'

'For finding Jasmine del Rio's body. That's really opened up the whole case for us.'

'Has it? You mean you think Jasmine killed Kenny and then topped herself?'

Detective Inspector Malik made a mock-tutting sound. 'I couldn't possibly make a statement like that before a lot more investigation has been completed, but I do finally think we're on the right track.'

So the authorities thought Jasmine del Rio was the murderer of Kenny Polizzi.

Charles Paris still somehow didn't.

Once the interview with Detective Inspector Malik was over it was too late for him to do anything except return to his digs and go to bed. But he got up early the next morning, the Wednesday, reckoning he had time before the *Cinderella* technical run started at ten to visit Vinnie McCree.

It was suddenly much colder, a reminder that November had given way to December. Ergh, Christmas approaching. He put the unwelcome thought from his mind. At least being in the pantomime meant there'd only be the one day – Christmas Day – to fill somehow.

Charles again noticed how quickly the well-maintained gentility of Eastbourne's tourist area gave way along Seaside Road to rows of increasingly shabby buildings. Taking his bearings from the Greyhound pub, he soon found the one in which Vinnie lived. In daylight it looked even less prepossessing. The white paint was flaked and mangy, the windows opaque with dust, a rusty ironing board and slumped black plastic bags of rubbish spilled over the tiny front garden. And the bell-pushes on the board by the front door had been repaired and replaced many times. Damp had caused the ink of the names in their little plastic pockets to run to illegibility.

But, as Charles was trying to remember which floor Vinnie's flat had been on, he noticed signs of more recent dilapidation. The front door was open. Splinters of bared wood around the lock suggested it had been forced. Charles pushed his way inside.

The two doors off the hall were firmly shut, and anyway he had a recollection of a drunken stagger down at least one flight of stairs when he left on the Tuesday morning. He made his way up the creaking staircase.

On the first-floor landing one door was closed but the other hung ajar. Again there were signs on the architrave that it had been forced. Charles went in.

Vinnie McCree lay on the floor in a flurry of newspapers. He had been shot in the forehead.

TWENTY

*BUTTONS: I've got a little secret, 'cause I'm just that kind
of feller.*
It's a secret I can only tell to Cinderella.

Charles Paris didn't call the police. He reckoned his finding three murder victims within six days might strain Detective Inspector Malik's tolerance. And though they'd parted the previous night on good terms, he really didn't fancy the inevitable further interrogation if he rang her with news of another murder.

He was confident he hadn't touched anything. He'd used his shoulder to push open the doors and kept his hand off the banister as he went up and down the stairs. He hadn't seen or, as far as he knew, been seen by anyone entering or leaving the house. Vinnie's was a body someone else could have the honour of finding.

But Charles's mind was full of questions. The main one being: why the hell would anyone want to kill Vinnie McCree? The man was a self-important old bore, but surely harmless.

And was the person who shot Vinnie the same one who had put paid to Kenny Polizzi? By now Charles was not even considering the possibility that Jasmine del Rio had committed the murder under the pier. The whole set-up of her suicide was too neat and convenient. He felt sure that when they investigated a little further, the police would find anomalies in the theory of Jasmine's guilt.

Unless, of course, Detective Inspector Malik was so pleased to have got a nice self-sealing explanation for the two deaths that she would discourage further enquiries.

The only solution that made sense to Charles was that Jasmine del Rio had been killed because she knew too much. Perhaps she had actually witnessed Kenny's murder, and for that reason the killer had to eliminate her?

Something similar might explain Vinnie's death too. Detective Inspector Malik said the journalist had supplied information about what he'd seen on the Friday night. Had he been another witness of the shooting?

Or had the killer found out that the police had been talking to Vinnie and shut him up permanently as a security measure?

That Wednesday they were no longer rehearsing in the St Asaph's Church Halls. For the first time they would be on stage at the Empire Theatre for the 'Tech' (as the technical run was always called). That would take as long as it took (which could be quite a long time) on the Wednesday and the Thursday morning. Then the plan was to have two dress rehearsals, one at two-thirty on the Thursday afternoon and the next at seven-thirty in the evening. These would set a template for the rest of the run, two performances a day until the middle of January, when mercifully the show would end.

Charles reckoned that *Cinderella* was way off the standard it should be for a show which would confront its first paying audience at the Friday matinee – even though that first audience would be all screaming kiddies. Bix Rogers was still devoting far too much of his time to the choreography, and though the introduction of Arthur Bodimeade had sharpened up the bits when the Ugly Sisters were on stage, there were still scenes not involving them which had hardly been rehearsed at all. Doctor Theatre – or some other actors' deity – was going to have to do an amazing transformation job on the show in the next two days.

Charles's mood was not improved when, arriving on time for the Tech, he was told by the stage management that Bix would be rehearsing out of sequence, doing all of the musical numbers first because 'the lighting for them is more complex'. Since the only musical number Baron Hardup was now involved in was the final Walkdown, it would be a while before Charles would be required for rehearsal. He was told to 'come back after lunch' and make sure he kept his mobile on in case the calls changed.

So a somewhat disgruntled Charles Paris went to check out the dressing room he would be sharing with a lot of other actors and decide what to do with the rest of his morning.

He felt very frustrated. The enquiry on which he had embarked now involved three murders, and yet he couldn't for the life of him see what he could do in the short term to further his investigation. He considered calling Lefty, but couldn't really think of anything to say. He'd decided it would be unwise to tell the lawyer about finding Vinnie's body. Let him hear the news through the official channels, through the police.

The one person Charles did want to talk to was Kitty Woo. She must by now have heard what had happened to Jasmine, and she'd be devastated. Charles wanted to offer her some kind of comfort – apart from confirming with her how unlikely Jasmine was ever even to contemplate suicide.

But, as he could hear through the tannoy in the dressing room, on stage the dancers were being put through their paces very hard by Bix. There wouldn't be an opportunity to talk to Kitty until one of the breaks – and during a Tech breaks could be fairly irregular.

He wandered disconsolately to the green room. The tannoy was turned up louder down there and he could hear the voice of Bix shouting at his lighting designer. Clearly it was going to be one of those Techs which ran and ran.

Felix Fisher, in pale green blouson and full make-up, was sitting in the corner with the *Times* crossword open in front of him. This made Charles feel slightly awkward. He had his own copy of the paper in the pocket of his duffel coat, but the crossword was a private thing for him. He was a bit anal about it, in fact, and didn't like being in the same room or railway compartment with someone else doing it.

'Hi,' he said casually.

'Hi, Charles. Both in the same boat, aren't we?' The comedian sounded peevish and upset. His manner was jittery. 'Called too early for rehearsal. First thing I've got to do is my version of "All By Myself" for the kitchen scene after Cinderella's gone off to the ball. No way Bix'll get to that till mid-afternoon.'

'I've got to wait even longer. If he is insisting on doing all the musical numbers first. Baron Hardup doesn't feature till the Walkdown.'

'Bix is such a disorganized prick!' snapped Felix Fisher waspishly. 'Do you fancy going out for a coffee?'

Charles looked at his watch. Not yet quarter past ten. They'd be hard pushed to find a pub open and it was a bit early, even for him. 'Yes, sure,' he said.

They ended up in the same coffee shop where he had been with Kitty and Laura Hahn. More familiar with the routine now, Charles ordered a double espresso. Felix, ordering a skinny latte, flirted camply with the male barista who recognized him 'from off the telly'.

'Presumably you heard about Jasmine,' said Charles, amazed that it was only the night before that he had discovered her body.

'Yes.' Felix sounded subdued. Charles wondered if it was Jasmine's death that had affected him. 'That kind of news travels really fast.'

'On Twitter again?'

'You bet.'

'And what are the Twitterists saying?'

'They tend to be called twitterati, Charles. And they're saying that Jasmine killed herself in remorse for having killed Kenny. Apparently there was a note of some kind.'

'But how on earth do they get the news so fast? It was only last night that . . .' Charles decided to gloss over his involvement in the discovery '. . . that her body was found. And I don't think there's been a police press conference about it yet.'

Felix shrugged. 'Some journalist may have got on to it. Possibly even a leak from the police . . . either an illegitimate one or deliberate? There's no secrecy anywhere any more. Once something's posted on Twitter the news goes round the world in no time.'

'I suppose so,' said Charles, the sum of whose knowledge of the workings of Twitter was not increasing. 'And would you buy that as an explanation?'

Another shrug. 'Well, until we get another more convincing one, it does seem to fit the known facts quite neatly.'

But what about the unknown facts? thought Charles. He didn't voice the question, though.

There was a natural hiatus in their conversation. Then Charles said, 'I think it's pretty shitty of the stage management to bring us in for ten. They could have texted us to say the rehearsal call was going to be later.'

'Don't blame the stage management. It's more likely Bix being shitty than them. I bet he only decided the rehearsal schedule when he arrived at the theatre this morning.'

'I hope at least someone got a message to Arthur Bodimeade not to hurry in. He looks so frail I think he should be conserving every drop of energy he's got.'

'Yes, but he is quite amazing when he gets into the routines, isn't he?' It was said slightly grudgingly, but it was praise, an *hommage* to the skills of an old generation that Charles would never have expected to hear from the abrasive young comic. 'And, actually, now I think of it, Danny said last night that neither he nor Arthur had been called this morning.'

'Oh? Then why couldn't someone have told us too?'

Charles's response was in no way loaded, but Felix seemed to think he needed to supply more information. 'The fact is, I went out for dinner with Danny last night.'

'Did you?'

'Yes, we had a very pleasant evening, bitching away about everyone.'

'Everyone in the *Cinderella* company?'

'Everyone in the theatre. And he reserved special venom for some of the guests he's had staying in his B&B. Astonishing how messy and destructive people can be when they're away from their own homes. He sees some really weird behaviour. They range from the predictable dirty weekenders who rattle the bedposts all night to one woman he mentioned who just spends all the time in her bedroom crying.'

'I don't envy him the job,' said Charles. The idea of letting strangers into anywhere he lived and then acting like a servant to them held no appeal.

'No.' Felix looked a little awkward as he said, 'And then Danny invited me back to his place for a nightcap . . . and I'm afraid I realized I had completely misinterpreted his intentions.'

'You mean he came on to you?'

'Yes, and how! He seemed to think that my agreeing to go back to his place for a nightcap meant I was agreeing to a whole lot more.'

'Oh dear.'

'It was acutely embarrassing because, you see . . .' The

stand-up was quiet for a moment, weighing up what he was about to say. 'Oh hell, I can tell you, Charles. The fact is, I've got to tell somebody.'

'Well, fine, if you want to. What is it?'

'The fact is, Charles . . . I am not gay.'

'Oh.' That did come as quite a shock, and Charles floundered a little for the proper response. 'Well, I mean, obviously that's up to you, but . . .'

'The trouble was when I was at university and started doing comedy I developed this gay persona and it went down really well. When I did straight stuff it didn't work. So then I take a show to Edinburgh and it's shortlisted for awards and stuff. And the more success I have, the more I'm kind of pushed into this gay ghetto. And it's fine because, though there are plenty of other gay stand-ups out there, the public can't seem to get enough of us. So there's plenty of work. I'd be daft to chuck up something that's really making me a very good living.

'But giving up the pretence and coming out as straight becomes more and more difficult. Because there's kind of a political element now involved. It's all right for Jews to do Jewish jokes, or Pakistanis to do Paki jokes. If someone else did them, that'd be racist. It's the same with the gay thing. I can do jokes about being a screaming queen because everyone thinks I am one. A straight man doing the same shtick would almost definitely be seen as homophobic. So I have got myself into a bit of a bind.'

'I can see that,' said Charles. 'And what about actual relationships? Does it mean you can't have any?'

Felix grinned ruefully. 'It means I have to be very discreet. Fortunately when I take off the make-up and the silly costumes nobody recognizes me, so I can have a kind of private life, if I'm careful. In fact . . .' He paused for a moment. 'Well, I've told you everything else, so I may as well tell you this too. I'm actually married with two small children.'

'Wow! A secret marriage. Very Wilkie Collins.'

'Exactly. Isn't it ridiculous, Charles?'

'It's odd, certainly. The exact reverse of how it used to be. I grew up with a generation of actors who had to keep their gay relationships secret, who had to pass off their partners as "flatmates" or "managers" or "chauffeurs". Yours is the first I've heard of working the other way round.'

'I just don't know how much longer I can keep it up, though,' said Felix glumly. 'The pressure gets worse and worse. I have to be so careful in interviews, in all dealings with the media. And I'm not sure that it really is fair on my wife, or the kids. I wouldn't mind getting out of the business completely, but the trouble is I make so much more money from stand-up than I could from anything else.'

'Hm.' There was a silence, then Charles asked, 'Why have you suddenly told me this?'

'Because I get the impression you're the kind of man who can keep a secret.'

'I hope that's true.'

'And because the pressure's getting worse and worse. That little scene with Danny last night was so embarrassing. I just had to tell someone. Also . . .' He ran out of words.

'What?'

'Well, this'll sound daft, Charles, but Danny was so furious last night . . . you know, because I wouldn't do what he wanted, that I got quite scared of him.'

'Did he attack you?'

'No. But he's a big man and I was afraid he was going to beat me up. He was threatening me with all kinds of things. Said I should watch my back if I was ever walking round Eastbourne after dark. And then he said something strange.'

'Oh?'

'He said: "Don't forget what happened to Kenny Polizzi, Felix. Something like that could easily happen to you too."'

'Did he?' said Charles Paris.

TWENTY-ONE

BUTTONS: The food in my B&B's terrible. Not very generous portions either. Last night at dinner my landlady asked, 'How did you find your steak?' I said to her, 'I moved a chip and there it was.'

Following the instructions Felix had given him, Charles had no difficulty finding Danny Fitz's house. It was in a small street off the landward side of Seaside Road, but not as far along as the squalid building where he'd found Vinnie McCree's body earlier that morning. Danny's was a red-brick cottage with windows and doors outlined in white stone. Probably late Victorian, possibly early Edwardian and considerably neater in appearance than its neighbours. Though no plants grew in them, the earth in the window-boxes on the ground floor sills was neatly raked, ready for the next season's planting. The front door's brass knocker, finger plate and surround of the bell-push had been polished to a high gloss.

A freshly painted sign beside the door read: 'DANMARK – Bed & Breakfast – All Rooms En Suite'. Charles wondered whether the house was just named after the Danish for 'Denmark', or if it was one of those composite words based on the owners' names. He had never thought before whether Danny Fitz might have a permanent partner. If such a person existed, it seemed a reasonable bet that he might be called Mark.

Charles hadn't planned what he was going to say to Danny, but he was too caught up in the excitement of his investigation to worry about that. Something, he felt sublimely confident, would come to him. He pressed his finger on the white centre of the bell-push.

Danny was mildly surprised, but not thrown to see him. He stepped back from the open doorway and said, 'Come in, Charles.'

There was just time for an impression of a hall lined with glass cases in which hung a meticulously arranged selection of pantomime dames' costumes before Danny said, 'I'm sure she's expecting you.'

'Oh yes, I'm expecting him,' said the voice of someone coming down the stairs.

Charles looked up to take in the unexpected sight of Gloria van der Groot. Behind thick glasses the skin around her eyes was puffy with much weeping.

And in her right hand she held a small automatic pistol.

TWENTY-TWO

*BUTTONS: First day I was in the B&B one of the chickens
died and we had chicken soup. Next day one of the pigs
died and we had pork chops. Third day the landlady's
old man was taken ill, so we went back home.*

Fortunately the actual threat of being shot didn't last very
long.

Danny Fitz stepped towards the stairs, announcing.
'There are very few rules at the Danmark B&B, but there are
some things not allowed on the premises under any circumstances.
They include whores, rent boys, inflatable women, copies of the
Daily Mail and, I'm afraid . . . guns.'

As he spoke the word he neatly picked the pistol out of Gloria's
hand. She offered little resistance.

'Anyway, where did you get this?'

'You got money, you can get anything. I learned that a long
time ago.'

Danny grunted. 'Well, I think I should make some coffee and
you two should go into the sitting room and have a little chat.'

He ushered them through. Gloria seemed numbed into obedi-
ence. Danny disappeared to the kitchen while the other two sat
down opposite each other.

Charles noticed that the sitting room too was a shrine to
pantomime memorabilia. Old programmes were displayed behind
glass. A giant rolling pin from some long-forgotten slapstick
kitchen scene stood in its own case. And pride of place was given
to a tall golden oriental headdress which Charles reckoned must
have been part of the Walkdown costume for Widow Twankey
in an *Aladdin* of many years before.

But these were momentary impressions. In his current predica-
ment Charles couldn't take much notice of his surroundings. He
was, after all, facing a woman who had recently threatened him
with a gun.

'I presume, Gloria,' he said, 'that it's you I have to thank for the texts saying I shouldn't be playing Baron Hardup.'

'Of course,' she said. 'That was Kenny's part.' Her voice wavered slightly, but there was no faltering in the confidence of her logic.

'I didn't take over the part out of any disrespect for him. I don't even think I would play it as well as Kenny would have done.' (This was a lie. Nearly every actor who takes over a part thinks they'll do it better than the previous incumbent.) 'But it's just the old showbiz thing – "The show must go on."'

'Why should it go on without Kenny? Nothing should go on without Kenny.'

Charles spoke gently. 'When did you originally' – he carefully avoided the words 'become obsessed with' – 'get interested in Kenny Polizzi?'

'When I saw the first episode of *The Dwight House*. I was just a teenager then, but I knew instinctively that I had to be near to him, in some way involved in his life.'

Charles did a quick mental calculation. If Gloria had been in her teens when the sitcom started, she must be a lot younger than he'd thought when he first saw her. He assumed she'd been round the fifty mark, her oddity perhaps exacerbated by menopausal symptoms. But now he had to revise that age to her late twenties.

'Did you tell anyone else how you felt, Gloria? Your parents?'

'What interest would it have been to them?' she asked sharply.

'They weren't people you could confide in?'

'God, no. If I had any problems, they only had one solution – give me more money. So pretty soon I stopped telling them if I had any problems.'

'Had they always had money?'

'My real father didn't have that much. They were comfortable, I guess, but no more than that. But then he died of a heart attack when I was, like, four.'

'I'm sorry.'

'So was I. And then a few years later my mom goes and marries this total asshole who's got money coming out of every orifice. And she wants me to start calling him "Pop" or "Daddy", and there's no way I'm going to do that.'

Their conversation was interrupted at this point by the arrival of Danny with a tray of coffee. As Charles found frequently when watching actors in domestic roles, Danny seemed to be giving a performance as a solicitous B&B owner.

'Gloria,' he said, 'I've put your gun in the house safe. I'm sorry, but those are my rules. I'll let you have it back when you leave – OK?'

Without much interest, Gloria agreed to these conditions. Then Danny said to Charles, 'I've been called for two this afternoon. What about you?'

'Same, but I wouldn't be surprised if we were to get a text telling us Bix is running late. I do think it's bloody daft rehearsing out of sequence when we're as close to opening as this.'

'Doesn't bother me too much. At least I know my routines with Arthur are rock solid. Anyway, I've got to do some shopping. So when you're done, if I'm not back the front door shuts on the latch. Just make sure it clicks to.'

'Will do.'

When Danny had gone, Charles said softly to Gloria, 'And when you first watched *The Dwight House* did you see a kind of relaxed family life totally unlike what you were experiencing at home?'

'Maybe,' Gloria replied shortly. 'I've never had much time for all that psychological garbage. I just saw a guy who was always going to be part of my life.'

'And since that time you tried to be wherever he was?'

'Yes. It's fairly easy to work out his schedule from stuff on his website and a lot of other showbiz and celebrity sites.'

'And you've never posed a threat to him?'

'Of course not, Charles. I love the guy.'

'Mm.' He was finding their conversation odd. Though Gloria was by most definitions a crackpot, when she spoke there was a compelling logic which seemed entirely natural. 'And now Kenny's dead . . .' That prompted a sparkle of tears behind the thick lenses '. . . what do you do now?'

'I don't know, Charles. That's what I don't know. I've thought of so many things.'

'Was shooting me one of those things?'

'Yes,' she replied with disarming frankness. 'I wanted revenge on someone, for what'd happened to Kenny. And when I heard from Danny that you were taking over the part of Baron Hardup, well, that seemed like it might be a start.'

Charles felt distinctly uncomfortable. Gloria was a crank, but not just a harmless crank. Shooting him would have seemed logical to her, and something she was quite capable of doing. He felt relieved to know that her pistol was safely locked away.

'So,' he asked, 'when did you first hear that Kenny Polizzi had been shot?'

'I didn't hear it,' she replied. 'I virtually saw it happen.'

TWENTY-THREE

FAIRY GODMOTHER: I'll give my magic wand a tap and
Then you'll hear what really happened.

This was the breakthrough Charles had been waiting for. He had spent so much of the last few days trying to piece together what had happened on the Friday night, and now he was in the presence of someone who might have witnessed all of it.

'Have you spoken to the police about what you saw?'

Gloria looked puzzled by the question. 'Why the hell should I do that?'

'Well, I think if someone's witnessed a murder it's fairly standard practice to report it to the cops.'

'This wasn't just any murder. This was the murder of Kenny Polizzi.'

'So what have you been doing since Friday evening?'

'I've been in my room right here, crying my eyes out. My life ended the moment Kenny was shot.'

'Yes, I can see it must have been hard for you. And have you thought of doing anything that might make you feel better?'

'Yes, I've thought of shooting the person who shot Kenny.'

'You know who he is?'

'I know what he looks like, but I'd never seen him before that night. I still can't put a name to him. Otherwise I'd have found him by now and killed him.' Again she made this sound a perfectly logical thing to do.

'Would you mind, Gloria,' asked Charles, 'just telling me exactly what did happen that Friday night?'

She thought for a moment, then said, 'Yeah, OK. You might be able to put a name to the bastard who killed Kenny.'

'So that evening, when did you start stalking—' Her expression showed she didn't like his choice of word, so he quickly corrected himself, '. . . following Kenny?'

'I waited around the rehearsal room, but he didn't come out at the end of the day like everyone else.'

'No.' Charles remembered. 'Kenny had been recording a chat show in London, so he wasn't called for rehearsal.'

'So, anyway, I then thought he might have gone to his hotel, so I went along to the Grand and waited around the foyer, and sure enough a car delivered him there round eight o'clock. And I felt good because that meant I'd seen him, and I like to see him every day. But I thought I'd hang around just to see if he might come out again. And he did – and I thought of speaking to him, but he had this really angry expression on his face. I know his moods very well and that would not have been a good time to talk to him.'

'I think he'd just come from a rather stormy encounter with Lilith Greenstone.'

'Ah, well, that would explain it, Charles. Lilith was never any good for him. The worst of all his wives. I was so mad when I heard he was marrying her. I knew it wouldn't work out.'

'So did you follow Kenny when he left the Grand?'

'Yes. He didn't see me. He was talking angrily into his cellphone. I wasn't close enough to hear what he was saying, but I think he was making arrangements to meet someone. And then, kinda midway between the Grand and the pier, this little car draws up alongside him, and Kenny gets into it.'

'What kind of car was it?'

'What do I know from cars?'

'Was it Mint Green?'

'I don't know about Mint, but it was pale green, yeah.'

Jasmine del Rio's Figaro, it must have been.

'Were you close enough to see the driver?'

'Not really, but I got the impression that it was a woman.'

'Mm. So did they drive off?'

'No, they stayed right there in the car.'

'For how long?'

'Five minutes tops. Then Kenny gets out and slams the door, like he's real pissed about something. And the car drives off, and he makes a call on his cellphone. Then he goes straight to a liquor store and comes out swigging from a vodka bottle. He sits on a bench with that for a while and then he makes a couple more calls on his cellphone. Then he goes into that pub, the one near the rehearsal room.'

'The Sea Dog.'

'Right.'

'And shortly afterwards I join him there.'

'Yes. Then after a while you both come out, and I don't know where you went, but Kenny heads for the pier. And he goes under the boardwalk and he meets this guy. Shabby, wearing this scruffy light-brown coat.' Vinnie McCree, thought Charles. 'I'm watching this from the side of a little cafe down there, so I can't hear what they're saying, but they seem to be doing some kind of deal. And the shabby guy goes and next thing Kenny's, like, snorting something out of a paper bag. Then he sits down at the foot of one of the pillars that hold up the pier and makes pretty serious inroads into the vodka bottle.'

'You still didn't think of going to talk to him then, Gloria?'

'No, Kenny was not a nice person when he'd been on the booze. He'd said some very hurtful things to me on occasions when he'd been drinking. What's more, down under the boardwalk he'd taken a gun out of his pocket and he was kind of fiddling with it. It wouldn't have been a good time to upset him.'

'So what happened next?' asked Charles.

'Well, I was thinking of coming back here, but then I didn't want to leave Kenny there in that state. You know, he might have got mugged or anything. So I wait. And it's getting quite late, no other people down at the beach level and very little traffic on the road above. Just the noise of the waves crashing against the shingle.

'Then I hear footsteps coming down the stairs from the pier entrance and this very slender blonde girl appears. And Kenny hears her feet on the shingle and he stands up and turns to face her.

'By now I've managed to get a bit closer and I can hear their words.

'The girl says: "So, Kenny . . . have you got something for me?"

'And he says: "Sure I've got something for you."

'And he raises his gun and shoots her in the forehead.'

TWENTY-FOUR

FIRST BROKER'S MAN: I've got the yaws – it's something chronic.
SECOND BROKER'S MAN: What's yaws?
FIRST BROKER: Well, thank you. Gin and tonic.

'What did you do?' asked Charles.

'Do? I stayed put. I wasn't going to let Kenny know I'd witnessed what just happened. He still had the gun, remember.'

'But what did you think, Gloria? When you saw this man you'd idolized shoot someone in cold blood?'

Kenny Polizzi's Number One Fan shrugged. 'I'm sure he had his reasons for doing it. The girl was hassling him about something.'

'It didn't make you think less of him?'

She looked at Charles as if he'd just asked the most peculiar question in the world. 'No. Of course not.'

'You didn't think of calling the cops?'

'Hell, no.'

'But you'd just witnessed a murder.'

'Yes, but artists like Kenny Polizzi can't be judged by the same standards as other people.'

Charles had heard that or similar lines on many occasions and they always made his blood boil. But now wasn't the moment to take issue. 'So what did Kenny do? Just leave the girl's body lying on the shingle?'

'No, first he made a call on his cellphone, but with the sound of the waves I couldn't hear what he was saying. Then he dragged her up to the steps that led up to the pier entrance. There was a big trash can there. He pushed the body out of sight behind it. Then he just waited, snorting more stuff from the paper bag, working his way down the vodka bottle.'

'Did he appear to be nervous or panicky?'

'No. He looked very calm. Anyway, after about ten minutes another man comes to join him.'

'Someone you recognized?'

Gloria shook her head. 'Never seen him before.'

'What did he look like?'

'Kinda short and round. With hair combed over his bald patch.'

It was the description Charles had been anticipating. Gloria went on, 'So the two of them talk briefly, then Kenny takes the other guy across to where the body is. And, each putting one of the dead girl's arms over their shoulders, they drag her up the steps to street level.

'I don't want them to see me, so I go up the steps the other side of the boardwalk. Parked outside the pier entrance is this little green car.'

'The one Kenny sat in earlier?'

'Yes. Or one identical to it. And there was a scary moment because just as Kenny and the other guy are manhandling the body to the car, a man walking his dog goes past.'

'How do they explain the body?'

'No problem as it turns out. The dog-walker says, "Ah. Another young lady had too much at the Atlantis." I don't know what he meant.'

'It's the nightclub at the end of the pier.'

'Oh. Anyway, the guy with the dog goes on, "In my young day women used to maintain their dignity." And he walks off, and the other two get the girl's body into the car.'

'Driving seat or passenger?' asked Charles, a vivid image coming to his mind of how he had found Jasmine del Rio's corpse.

'Passenger seat. Then Kenny and the other guy go back down to the beach.'

'Do you follow them?'

'No. I wait at street level. I want to see where the car's going.'

'Do you have to wait long?'

'No. The other guy, the guy I don't recognize, he comes up, gets into the green car with the girl's body beside him and drives off.'

'So did you follow the car?'

'No, I was on foot.'

'Then how did you know where he'd left the car?'

'I had no idea where he—'

'But you sent me an anonymous text.'

'I sent you two texts saying you shouldn't take over Kenny's part – that's all.'

Charles Paris's mind was racing with new thoughts, but there were other facts he had to establish first. 'So, after the car's been driven off, then you go back down to the beach to see Kenny?'

'Yes. Then I go back down to the beach and find Kenny dead.'

TWENTY-FIVE

FAIRY GODMOTHER: Now all is clear – so all is fine –
To the meanest intellect.
FIRST BROKER'S MAN: But what about mine?

As he left the Danmark B&B, Charles checked his watch. Still not twelve o'clock. Time for a little more investigation before his rehearsal call. Though in fact he was now so caught up in the case, he would have allowed nothing – even his first night as King Lear at the National Theatre – to put him off the chase.

What he had heard from Gloria van der Groot had filled in an enormous number of holes in his reconstruction of the previous Friday night. But there were still important details missing. Details which could only be provided by Kenny Polizzi, Vinnie McCree or Lefty Rubenstein. And of the three, the lawyer had the enormous advantage of still being alive.

Charles rang his cellphone number. And yes, Lefty was at his hotel. And yes, he'd be happy to meet Charles. In the bar, same as on the Sunday.

There were a few more people this time, men and women in business suits drinking coffee, all with ID cards hanging from lanyards round their necks. The hotel was clearly hosting a conference. And all the delegates seemed to be speaking in some lilting Scandinavian language. The Christmas tree was now decorated, but that did little to animate the room.

Lefty was already sitting at a table with the inevitable bottle of Diet Coke in front of him. Because of the conference delegates, there actually was a barmaid in attendance this time. Charles just ordered a double espresso. He wanted to have his wits about him.

'So what is it, Charles?' asked Lefty. 'You reckon you've solved Kenny's murder?'

'I think I could be closer to a solution.'

'Great. And, as per our agreement, you've come to share your findings with me.'

'That's pretty much it, yes.'

'So can I ask if there was something, some big breakthrough, that made it all clear to you?'

'There was, I suppose. You know we talked about a woman called Gloria van der Groot?'

'Sure. Kenny's Number One Fan.'

'She's still here in Eastbourne.'

'Really? I thought she'd gone back to the States.'

'Well, she hasn't.'

'It's no surprise she came here, though. Everywhere Kenny went, Gloria van der Groot was not far behind him. But I think she's harmless. Kenny always said she was harmless.'

'I wouldn't be completely convinced about that. Within the last couple of hours she's pulled a gun on me.'

'What'd you done to upset her?'

'Taken over the part of Baron Hardup. Taken over Kenny's part.'

'Oh yeah. Well, I guess to someone as unhinged as her that could definitely count as grounds for murder. Congratulations on the fact that she didn't succeed.'

'Thank you. But Gloria did have some very interesting stuff to tell me about Friday night.'

'Uh-huh?'

'She doesn't like being called a stalker, but what she did on Friday amounted to stalking.'

'You mean she followed him?'

'Yes.'

'For how long?'

'Most of the evening.'

'Ah.' The reaction was light, but Charles reckoned it signalled a new wariness in Lefty's manner. 'What did she see?'

'She saw Kenny get into Jasmine del Rio's car.'

'This would be early on. Before he took up his pitch under the boardwalk?'

'Yes.'

'Presumably Gloria couldn't overhear the conversation Kenny and Jasmine had inside the car?'

'No. But I have a pretty good idea of what they discussed.'

'Enlighten me.'

'Jasmine was blackmailing Kenny. You'd paid her off in LA when she threatened to spill the beans about him screwing her when she was under-age. She reckoned, now their paths had crossed again, there was more money where that came from.'

'You're right. And her rates had certainly gone up. She was asking for fifty thousand pounds, "for starters".'

'And did Kenny ask you to get the money together that evening?'

'No, no, Charles. Miracle worker I may be, but there are limits. My advice was we play it cool. Set up a meeting for the three of us the next day, work out some kinda compromise. Negotiate.'

'But Kenny was in no mood to negotiate?'

'I found that out later. For that evening I reckoned my work was done. I'd organized the cocaine he'd asked for, set up this old creep to hand the stuff over to him under the pier and advised him about Jasmine del Rio. I reckoned I deserved an early night.'

'But you didn't get one?'

'No. Not as things turned out.'

It was suddenly quiet in the bar. The Scandinavians' coffee break was over and they'd returned to another session of their conference. The barmaid had gone too.

'Kenny called you later?'

'Yes. He was kinda hysterical . . . you know, with the booze and the coke, but there was also something gleeful in his manner. Gleeful like he was proud of himself, like he'd done something very clever.'

'What exactly did he say?'

'He said he'd sorted out "that little blackmail problem". Then he told me how he'd done it.'

'By shooting Jasmine del Rio?'

'Yup. And then he says I've got to go and tidy up for him. He actually said to me, "You've always been good as a Pooper-Scooper, Lefty."' He tensed, clearly loathing the expression.

'He was asking you to clear up the body after he'd committed a murder?'

'Yes, that's exactly what he was doing. Kenny thought he was above the law. Any scrape he got into, he only had to pick up the phone, call Lefty. Lefty'd tidy things up. Lefty'd see to it no unpleasantness might attach to Kenny Polizzi. God, I was used to it. That was the way he'd treated me right through our professional relationship. But what got to me was . . . he couldn't see the fact that murder was on a different scale from all his other misdemeanours.'

'So you worked out how you were going to get rid of Jasmine's body?'

'Yes. To set it up to look like suicide seemed to me the easiest way. I mean it's not like Eastbourne's a town I know well. Back in LA, I got contacts. I could find people with experience of that kind of work. But I reckoned putting the body in the car and leaving it someplace was going to be the best way. It was just sheer luck that I found that lock-up to put the car in. I was never reckoning it'd be a long time before the body was found. And when I felt the police were being a bit slow, I decided to give them a nudge.'

'The anonymous text sent to my mobile. The one that mentioned Ranleigh Road. At first I thought that must have come from Gloria. Now I realize it was you.'

'Yes, I sent it. I knew you were a keen sleuth hound, Charles. You'd be on to it straight away. You'd find the body. And you'd probably read the clues I'd left and come to a private verdict of suicide.'

'Of course what's odd, though, Lefty, is the reason why she appeared to have killed herself. It was out of remorse for having killed Kenny Polizzi. And yet at the time her body was being put into her car to be driven away, Kenny was still very much alive.'

Lefty swallowed down the last of his Coke and looked with annoyance towards the unmanned bar. Then he said, 'You've worked it out, haven't you, Charles?'

'It's the only solution that fits the facts. You shot Kenny Polizzi, didn't you, Lefty?'

The lawyer let out a long sigh. Then he brushed a rueful hand across his comb-over. 'Yes, I did. All my working life Kenny had been piling more and more straws on me. That was the one that broke my back. Asking me to tidy up after a murder . . .

no, I couldn't do it. And all of the humiliations that had been building up over the years . . . it's like they all came rushing back into my memory, and at that moment I hated Kenny. Hated him more than I had ever hated anyone in my life.

'So when we'd got the girl's body in the car we went to the beach again to check whether anything of hers had been left down there, and Kenny just stood there grinning at me. Grinning. I'd done everything and he was the one who seemed to think himself clever. He also didn't seem to see that shooting that girl was different from anything he'd done before. "Oh dear, I've managed to do something stupid. Never mind, Lefty Rubenstein will come and clear up after me. He always does. That's what I pay him for."

'When Kenny'd finished wiping the pistol with a handkerchief to remove any traces of his fingerprints, he was still grinning.

'And then he handed the gun across to me, and as he did so, he said, "Where would I be without my Pooper-Scooper?" And I don't know, I've always hated being called that. Lots of other insulting things he'd called me over the years, they didn't worry me. But that . . . And I suddenly saw how logical it would be, how many of my hassles and aggravations would be solved by the one simple act. I raised the pistol until the end of the barrel was resting against his forehead.

'Kenny was still grinning when I pulled the trigger.'

There was a long silence. 'And after that,' said Charles, 'you set up Jasmine's supposed suicide and turned all the suspicion on her?'

'Uhuh. I had been walking round earlier in the week and I found the empty lock-up. I always look out for stuff like that – never know when you're going to need it. And it was a good place because I knew her body would be discovered pretty soon. All very easy . . . well, except for managing the gear stick on that little toy car of hers. Why you Brits don't come into the twenty-first century and have automatics I'll never know.

'But my disposal of the girl's body was quite neat, I thought, even though I say it myself. Kinda thing you learn how to do if you're raised on the back streets of LA. And of course if you've trained as a lawyer.'

After this little half-joke, Lefty suddenly stood up, crossed to the bar and banged the bell for service. When the barmaid appeared he ordered another Diet Coke. 'Another coffee, Charles?'

'I think I'll go for a large Bell's this time. Just with ice.'

When Lefty was back sitting down, Charles asked, 'And how do you feel now?'

The lawyer opened his hands in a gesture of non-commitment. 'How should I feel?'

'Did it work? Once Kenny was dead, did you really find all your hassles and aggravations had been resolved?'

'For a time I did feel that, yes. When I'd sorted out the girl in the car, I felt a kind of closure. I'd discharged my last duty for the bastard. Never again would I have to clean up one of Kenny Polizzi's messes. It was over. At last I could get on with my own life.'

'But you don't still feel that, do you, Lefty?'

The lawyer looked straight into Charles's eye. 'You're not a bad psychologist. Maybe you should give up this acting game and put up your shingle as a shrink.'

'Might not work. There's a big difference between being a good psychologist and a good psychiatrist.'

'Yup, you're right.' Charles allowed the silence to flow before Lefty said, 'I was, like, euphoric after I'd done it. I'd got rid of Kenny. Finally the monkey was off my back.'

'But the euphoria didn't last . . .?'

'No. No, it didn't.'

'Are you worried about being investigated by the police, Lefty?'

'No way. With the girl's suicide and the note on her cellphone, they're not going to be looking a lot further. If there's one thing police like all over the world it's an open-and-shut case.'

'But suppose there was a witness, suppose someone did see you actually shooting Kenny?'

'Why, was there a witness?' he asked, alarmed.

'Not so far as I know.'

'Good.'

'But the police have other resources. How would you feel if they did actually nail you for the crime?'

Lefty looked out of the window, towards the thin rectangle of sea visible between buildings. 'Do you know, Charles, I wouldn't mind that much. It wouldn't be such a big deal for me. OK, professional pride hurt a bit, because I'd've failed to set up the perfect murder . . . but otherwise . . . no, if they nailed me, full marks to the police.'

'Presumably, with your legal expertise, you'd mount a pretty good defence?'

'Yes, I suppose I might. Then again I might not. I really don't care any more. You see, I've got Kenny out of my life, and that should have solved all of my problems. Because without Kenny's constant unreasonable demands, I can go back to being Lefty Rubenstein. Running my legal practice for me, like I did before I ever got involved with Kenny Polizzi. I should be happy about that.

'But I'm not. After a couple of days of feeling good – yeah, like I said, the euphoria – I woke up on Monday morning and I thought: what the hell am I going to do? How'm I going to fill the day? And the next day? And all the days after that?

'I realize that without Kenny hassling me, I have no motivation to do anything. He'd kinda consumed me. There wasn't any of the original Lefty Rubenstein left. Yes, Kenny drove me mad, but without him, I'm on my way to getting madder. And it's more than that . . . I actually *miss* the guy.

'You know, Charles,' said Lefty, his eye still locked on its glimpse of the sea, 'I think, in my own strange way, I actually loved Kenny.'

Charles Paris was of the view that he didn't need to share Lefty's confession with Detective Inspector Malik. He felt sure the police would get there in their own time. Detailed forensic examination of Jasmine's Figaro was bound to punch great holes in the theory that she had committed suicide. And once that was out of the way, there was no longer any logical reason to finger her as Kenny Polizzi's murderer.

As it worked out, the official police investigation received a boost from further events of that afternoon. Unbeknown to Charles, after he had left the Danmark Bed & Breakfast, Danny had returned from his shopping. Gloria had got into conversation with her host about Kenny and his entourage. Danny had spoken of Lefty and his description of the agent made Gloria sure that he had been the unknown man who had joined Kenny under the pier.

Danny had left a copy of the *Cinderella* stage management's contact sheet around. Lefty was listed there, along with most of the artistes' agents. It also gave the number of the hotel where he was staying.

Gloria, saying she felt better and must really organize her return flight to the States, packed, paid Danny what she owed him and, as agreed, was allowed to take her automatic pistol from the safe.

Once out of the Danmark Bed & Breakfast, she walked briskly along Seaside Road until she arrived at Lefty's hotel. She sat quietly in the foyer until, mid-afternoon, he emerged from the lift.

Then Gloria van der Groot shot him dead.

TWENTY-SIX

*AT THE END OF THE WALKDOWN, CINDERELLA AND
   PRINCE CHARMING ENTER IN THEIR WEDDING
   CLOTHES.*
*PRINCE CHARMING: So all is well, and naught's
   alarming . . .*
CINDERELLA: Now Cinderella's wed Prince Charming!

The Tech for *Cinderella* overran horribly, as Techs will, and the proposed two dress rehearsals on the Thursday ended up being reduced to one. There is an old adage, much believed among theatricals, that 'a bad dress rehearsal presages a good opening', but at the end of the Thursday evening most of the *Cinderella* company were agreed that a dress rehearsal that bad must presage a seriously shitty opening.

Charles wasn't quite so pessimistic. As a punter, he would have come to see the show for Danny Fitz and Arthur Bodimeade's routines alone. He loved participating in the ones which involved Baron Hardup and the ones where he wasn't onstage he watched avidly from the wings.

But lack of rehearsal – apart from other stresses of the previous few days – meant that on the Friday he woke early and twitchy. He knew from experience that doing one's first performance to a horde of screaming kiddies was a mixed blessing. They might not be as aware of onstage cock-ups as adults, but they had a distressing variety of reactions to demonstrate that they were bored. Charles had spent more than one children's matinee being pelted with salted peanuts.

(Other missiles were popular too. There used to be a panto-mime tradition that at a given point in every performance 'sweeties' were thrown out into the auditorium to be grabbed for by overenthusiastic children. But as they have to so many sources of innocent pleasure, Health and Safety put a stop to that. Charles Paris didn't mind, actually. He remembered one schools matinee of *Little Red Riding Hood* when the audience, not liking the 'sweeties' that they were being offered, started throwing them back at the cast. With remarkable power and accuracy. Charles had had to play the rest of the run with a black eye.)

On that Friday morning there was to be a company call at twelve 'for notes', which meant Bix knew he'd reached the point when no more tinkering would make the show any better. Some of the company were no doubt making or shopping for first performance presents, but such gestures were a bit too theatrical for Charles Paris.

So he twitched around his digs, nibbling some stale toast and trying to convince himself that the afternoon would be all right.

And then he had a phone call from Detective Inspector Malik. She would like to talk to him.

He explained that he had to be in the theatre for twelve, so she suggested they should meet in the coffee shop near the stage door. She sounded unnervingly affable.

But her first question when they met was full of suspicion. 'Mr Paris, what were you doing at the flat of Vinnie McCree on Wednesday morning?'

Oh dear. So he had been seen there.

'Well, I wanted to see him,' he said feebly.

'Why?'

'You'd mentioned the day before that you'd talked to him and I . . .'

'You didn't get the chance to talk to him, did you?'

'No, I found him dead in his room.' He searched for comfort in Detective Inspector Malik's black eyes. 'How did you know I was there? Did someone see me?'

'There were surveillance cameras set up opposite the house.'

'Police surveillance?'

'No, they were set up by the other side.'

'Other side?'

'Very fortunate for us, as it turns out.'

Charles was finding the conversation a little gnomic. 'I'm sorry, I don't quite get what you mean.'

'Well, the fact is that the drug scene here in Eastbourne – there's always been one, but it's been fairly low key, almost a cottage industry. But now some of the Albanian gangs who operate in other south-coast towns are trying to muscle in. They're the ones who set up the surveillance cameras. And thereby produced a great deal of evidence for us.'

'Why did they set the cameras up, though?'

'They were suspicious of Mr McCree. He'd been asking too many questions about their operations. So they wanted to see who his associates were.'

'So they'd also have seen you when you visited him at the house too, wouldn't they? Police cars . . . they wouldn't have liked that.'

'No. I think that's possibly why they decided that he was a threat to their security.'

'Why they shot him, in fact?'

'It's possible,' she said without any hint of guilt. 'But of course we could never have known that was going to happen. I think Mr McCree did behave foolishly, though. He got in rather deeper than he intended.'

Charles agreed. Though he couldn't help feeling a level of pity for Vinnie McCree. Silly, pathetic old fool, still thinking he could come up with the career-driving scoop. And ending up being executed by an Albanian drug-trafficker.

Then a rather unpleasant thought came to him. 'If I'm caught on their surveillance cameras, then these Albanians might think I'm one of Vinnie's associates and . . .'

Detective Inspector Malik smiled. 'Down worry about it, Mr Paris. The good thing about recent events is that they've opened up this Albanian connection. We've arrested the lot of them.'

'Oh, well done,' said Charles, with considerable relief. 'And, er, what about the other murders?'

'The other murders?'

'Well, we've had quite a succession of them now, haven't we? You know, connected with *Cinderella*. First Kenny Polizzi, then Jasmine del Rio, then—'

'Mr Paris . . .'

'Yes?'

'I think we in the police force are quite capable of sorting out any connections there may be between those crimes.'

'Oh yes. I'm sure you are. I wasn't suggesting that . . . It's just, I mean, I did know the people involved and if you needed any, as it were . . .'

'I'm sure you did, Mr Paris. And I'm sure if we reach a point when we need help in joining the dots on the case, you'll be the first person we'll get in touch with.'

'Oh well, thank you.'

'But don't hold your breath.'

Detective Inspector Malik didn't call him again, so Charles reckoned the police had worked out exactly what happened with what became known as the '*Cinderella* shootings'.

And a long time later (the wheels of justice turn slowly) he saw in *The Times* that Gloria van der Groot had been committed to a secure institution. But he never knew that she spent her time there very happily, watching continuous box sets of *The Dwight House*.

That series got a boost from the publicity surrounding the murder. Like Elvis's, as Lefty Rubenstein had predicted, Kenny Polizzi's death had proved 'a good career move'.

And a large percentage of the international royalties from the show went to Lilith Greenstone who, at the time of his death, was still Kenny's wife. Her career continued to blossom, but in spite of road-testing a lot of men in her bed, Lilith still didn't find what she was looking for.

Cinderella did open on time for the Friday matinee to an auditorium full of screaming kids. It wasn't the greatest performance ever, but the company got through it. The evening show was trickier. An adult audience was less forgiving to the longueurs of the set changes and the gaping holes in the plot. But, as Danny Fitz kept saying, 'First week of performances in pantomime is always like the third week of rehearsal.'

And slowly the show took shape. The cast began to feel the rhythms of the story and it shook down into not a bad little show. Even more remarkably, a couple of the local newspapers praised Bix's direction, describing it as 'tight and lively'. There was only

one review for Baron Hardup. 'Charles Paris looked as if he'd
wandered in from another show (and would rather be back there).'
Eastbourne Herald.

And in time the various lives of the *Cinderella* company took
various directions. Kitty Woo, desolated by the loss of Jasmine
del Rio, began to see quite a lot of Laura Hahn. United in their
grief, a mutual attraction grew. Neither wanted to move too fast,
both were wary, but maybe in time something might develop
there.

After much toing and froing, and many misgivings, as soon
as he'd finished the run of *Cinderella*, Felix Fisher came out
as straight. He couldn't any longer stand the pressure of
keeping his wife and children secret. And to his amazement,
the revelation had exactly the effect that his career needed.
Within six months he was hosting a family-friendly television
quiz.

Arthur Bodimeade died within a fortnight of *Cinderella*'s last
performance. But during the run he hadn't missed a single show
and, though there were only a few of them, connoisseurs of the
theatre sat in the auditorium of the Empire Theatre, realizing
they were in the presence of genius.

And Charles Paris . . . For him life chuntered on. The shock
of hearing about Frances's potential illness, the reminder that
one day he might lose her, had affected him deeply. But not
deeply enough for him to arrange to see her more often. Or even
to ring her more often.

He did, however, get through to her between the matinee and
the evening show on Christmas Eve.

'Frances, just rang to wish you a Happy Christmas.'

'That's very thoughtful of you,' she said with just the slightest
edge to her voice. 'Happy Christmas to you too.'

'I assume you'll be spending tomorrow with Juliet and Miles?'

'Yes. I'm sure, if you had got in touch earlier, you'd have been
very welcome to—'

'Couldn't have done it. We only get tomorrow off, then two
shows again on Boxing Day. And what with there being no trains
on Christmas Day . . .'

'So what will you be doing tomorrow?'

He was encouraged to hear concern in her voice. 'Oh, I'm sure I'll find something to do.'

'Joining up with some other people from the *Cinderella* company?'

'Something like that, yes.' Though he hadn't discussed plans with anyone.

'And I'm sorry, Frances. I haven't got you a present. It'll have to be in the New Year.'

'I'm used to that, Charles.'

'Yes.'

There was a silence. Then Frances said, 'I have got quite a lot of present-wrapping and stuff to be getting on with, so I . . .'

'Yes, yes, of course. I just wanted to say, about the breast cancer . . .'

'The good news is that I haven't got breast cancer.'

'Yes, but I just wanted to say . . . you know, the scare, when I thought you might have it . . . well, it made me realize how much you do still mean to me . . . how upset I'd be if something were to happen to you.'

'I'd be pretty pissed off too,' said Frances, deliberately lightening the tone.

'And I'd just like to say, coming up to New Year and resolutions and all that . . .'

'Keeping resolutions has never been one of your strong points, Charles.'

'No, I know.' He took a moment to build up his courage and then asked in a rush, 'But shall we make next year the year we see a lot more of each other?'

'I don't know, Charles. Shall we?' She didn't sound convinced.

He did find a pub that was open at lunchtime on Christmas Day. Only serving drinks. The ones doing a full Christmas lunch had all been booked up weeks before. But when everyone was turned out of the pub at three in the afternoon, Charles found a convenience store open and bought some stuff, took it back to his self-catering digs, and self-catered.

He got through the day.

Thereafter, as long as he was in Eastbourne, he just got on with the show. And twice a day, along with Nausea, Dyspepsia and

Buttons, Baron Hardup watched as the sheet of words came down from the flies, and they all encouraged the audience to join in the community singing.

Smile if you're happy, smile if you're not.
Smile if you're in clover, or if you're in a spot.
If you want to be in style,
Just make sure you always smile.
So for the world of worries we could not care a jot.
Life for us is lovely and we're happy with our lot!
(RALLENTANDO)
Life for us is lovely and – we're – happy – with – our – lot!,

Lightning Source UK Ltd.
Milton Keynes UK
UKHW040819290819
348753UK00006B/14/P